JOE

ROBINSON

by

Carol Lea

 New Generation Publishing

For Gam and my four lovely grandchildren
Poppy, Noah, Rachel and Isabel.

Chapter 1

Roddy Johnson was mindful of the peak hour traffic ahead and alongside him as he cycled the six miles from his flat to Southlands School. His student debt meant that he couldn't afford a car, but he consoled himself by thinking at least he was reducing his carbon footprint and saving a fortune in gym membership. He was frustrated by the number of cars intruding into the cycle lane to avoid being held up. He had nearly reached the school when a large black Range Rover suddenly cut across his path. If he hadn't been alert, Roddy would have been knocked off his bicycle. To avoid a collision he was forced to veer off the main road into a side road. The driver had been using his mobile phone and was probably unaware of the accident he had nearly caused.

As he was turning his bicycle back towards the main road, something further down the side road caught his eye. Two bulky figures were surrounding a much smaller, ginger haired boy and were obviously trying to take something from him. Without a moment's hesitation, Roddy jumped off his bike and ran towards them, at the same time yelling, 'Oi, you two, leave him alone! Pick on someone your own size!' The bullies took one look at Roddy's 6′ 3″ athletic body charging towards them and immediately ran off.

'Are you all right?' Roddy asked the boy who looked pale and shaken by the ordeal. He nodded and smiled bravely before thanking him.

'I can see from your uniform that you're a pupil at Southlands School. I'm going there too as it happens so I'll walk the rest of the way with you.' Roddy picked up his bicycle and walked it along the pavement while talking to the boy. 'Did they take anything?'

'No, not really. They just took a Mars bar. I think you arrived just in time so they didn't get my dinner money. I didn't bring my mobile phone today and I think that's what they were after.'

'Good. Is it your first day at Southlands?'

'Yes.'

Roddy had guessed from his size and brand new uniform. 'Well, it's not a very good start for you. It's my first day too as it happens.... So we're both new boys! I'm Roddy Johnson, by the way, and I'll be teaching English and Drama. What's your name?'

'Harry Smyth. It's actually Harry Cowper-Smyth, but I think it's best if I'm just called Harry Smyth.'

'Why's that?' Roddy asked, although he already knew the answer.

'My father's the local M.P. and I want to keep quiet about that. Anyway Cowper-Smyth sounds a bit posh doesn't it?' Roddy could only smile in agreement. 'It didn't matter at my last school as there were plenty of other boys with posh sounding names.'

'Really? Which school was that?'

'It was a boarding school in Cumbria, but I didn't like it at all.'

'I can understand that. It's tough being away from home at your age. Don't you have any brothers or sisters?'

Harry shook his head. 'No. I don't know anyone at the school either, but I'm hoping to make some new friends.'

'I'm sure you will. You seem a nice young man to me!' Roddy said, trying to bolster his confidence. He felt sorry for the boy who was polite and well spoken and had an angelic, choirboy face. He wondered how well Harry would be able to integrate into the new school and sensed his unease as they got nearer to the school gates. 'Don't let those thugs put you off. I've heard that the school has a strict policy on bullying so you must report any incidents. I'd better be off now. I don't suppose you want to be seen coming into school with a teacher.' As he prepared to mount his bike, he turned to Harry and smiled warmly. 'One last thing, I'll not tell anyone your real name as long as you don't tell anyone my name is Rodney!' They both laughed before Roddy cycled off in the direction of the school gates.

Southlands School was set back from the main road, with a bus turnaround outside the gates and a large blue sign with the name of the school and the headmaster Mr. A. Atkinson, featuring prominently in white lettering. A long driveway split into two before the main entrance. One branch to the left led to the car park and the other, to the right, led to the bike sheds, playground and sports pitches beyond.

Harry was already vaguely familiar with the layout of the school, as his parents had taken him to an Open Evening with displays of work and various activities across the whole school. The Open Evening had included a speech to prospective pupils and parents by the headmaster, Alex Atkinson, who commanded respect as soon as he walked on the stage. He was tall and strongly built, with neat, grey hair and wore a gown over his suit. His booming voice mesmerized the audience and needed no microphone to reach the back of the hall. He pointed out the school's outstanding Ofsted Report and proudly listed the school's successes as if it was all his own achievement. He had an inflated ego and longed to be recognised with Super Head status so he was more concerned with enhancing his own reputation than giving credit to anyone else. None of the parents who attended the Open Evening could fail to be impressed by Mr Atkinson.

'He certainly knows how to talk the talk,' Martin Cowper-Smyth muttered to his wife Alice as they left the school.

'I can see why he has a reputation as a strict disciplinarian. I was frightened of him myself!' Alice laughed.

'What did you think of him Harry?'

'He was a bit scary but I suppose that's a good thing in a headmaster.'

'So how do you feel about the school?'

'It seems a very good school to me and I could walk there from our house. It's probably not worth looking at any other school.'

'Well, that sounds like it's settled then,' Martin smiled at his son.

Months later, Harry relived their conversation in his mind as he joined the stream of new pupils making their way up the main pathway to the school. He wondered how his parents might react if he told them about the attack and how it would change their opinion of the school.

Some of the pupils were congregating on the paved area in front of the main entrance, waiting for other friends to join them. Harry listened to the excited chatter all around him and envied their friendship. As an only child he should have been used to being on his own. He had always found it difficult to make friends and at his last school he had struggled to feel accepted. He had felt like an outsider, an onlooker rather than a participant in the other boys' games. He had been given the nickname *Red Harry* and was teased mercilessly because of his ginger hair and his father's occupation as a Labour politician. However, he was determined that things would be better at his new school and pushed aside these negative thoughts.

A staggered start meant that there were only Year 7 pupils in school until 11 o'clock, apart from prefects in their distinctive maroon jumpers. The Year 7 pupils were easily recognised because of their mainly brand new uniforms: brilliant white shirts or blouses, navy blazers or jumpers that seemed slightly too large for them, immaculate trousers or skirts and shiny, unscuffed shoes. Harry studied the squeaky clean youngsters around him and wondered if any of them were feeling the rising panic and apprehension that was churning his stomach into knots. He tagged on the end of one of the crocodiles of youngsters being led by prefects into the main hall. He was then directed to one of the rows of chairs allocated for his form, 7S, and was greeted by his form teacher, Mr Pearson. Nigel Pearson was a round faced, tubby little man with an extremely shiny, baldhead. His short legs were engulfed by baggy trousers that drooped in folds around his ankles, swamping his small feet.

After an assembly Harry and the rest of 7S followed Mr Pearson to his teaching room that was to be their form room for the next school year. The pupils jostled to be as near to the back of the class as possible, but Harry headed instead for the desk the others avoided, on the front row, directly opposite the teacher's desk. When all of the pupils had found their seats, the chair next to Harry remained empty.

One of the girls in the desk behind Harry kicked his chair to attract his attention. Turning around, he was surprised to see a pretty, friendly looking girl beaming at him with a huge smile that seemed to light up her face. She had short brown hair, cut in a bob, and brown, almond shaped eyes and sitting next to her was an equally attractive girl with shoulder length, wavy, blonde hair and deep blue eyes.

'Hi, I'm Poppy and she's Rachel. What's your name?'

'Harry Smyth.'

'Thought you looked a bit lonely on your own. Haven't you got any friends here?' Poppy asked with genuine concern.

'No, I haven't. My last school was in Cumbria so I don't know anyone.' Harry didn't reveal till much later, when they were good friends, that it was a boarding school.

'Don't you know any kids from your street?' Poppy persisted.

'No. Not really. Most of the people who live on our street are retired or have their meals delivered by Meals on Wheels! A lot of houses have been converted into flats for people without children.'

Poppy and Rachel sniggered at his description. 'Oh, I see what you mean!' Poppy exclaimed. 'I would hate that. Rachel and I live next door to each other and we're always popping into each other's houses. Our mums are friends and we've been best friends forever. Haven't we Rachel?'

Rachel nodded and looked down shyly. She twirled her hair nervously around her finger and seemed happy to let Poppy do all the talking. Harry wondered how the two girls had become friends, as they seemed so different. Poppy was very talkative and, once started, was like an express train that couldn't be stopped. Harry found himself drawn by her friendly magnetism and bubbly personality. He also liked Rachel but she was much more quiet and reserved and took longer to make friends. He wasn't used to talking to girls; they were an alien species to him and he usually felt awkward around them. But he didn't feel uncomfortable talking to Poppy; she was an expert at teasing out reluctant conversation. Her eyes seemed to smile and see straight through him, reading him like a book. Somehow she guessed that he was an only child and she stated, rather than asked the question, 'You don't have any brothers or sisters, do you.'

'No. I don't,' Harry confirmed. 'I wish I had.'

'Well, you are welcome to tag along with us if you like. It's not much fun being on your own,' Poppy kindly offered and looked towards Rachel.

Rachel promptly shrugged her shoulders and said, 'We don't mind.'

'Thanks.' Harry smiled back at them. He was glad to have made some new friends but wished they were boys rather than girls.

'We've got lots of friends who are boys,' Poppy gushed. 'You might have gathered I'm a bit of a tomboy. Rachel is as well, but not as much as me. I've never liked playing with dolls or wearing a dress. I'm far happier wearing jeans and kicking a football.' Poppy was in full flow but was stopped in her tracks by Mr Pearson who called the class to order. Harry had to turn around and there wasn't much chance to talk after that.

The remaining 45 minutes of form time were taken up with registration, checking contact details, making copies of the timetable and homework timetable and distribution of homework diaries. The latter was greeted with much moaning and groaning. Harry was delighted to find that Mr Johnson would be teaching the class for both English and Drama and that Mr Pearson would be teaching them for History. When the class were asked if anyone could guess why the forms were named 7S, 7T, 7H, 7L, 7N and 7D, Harry, with his usual reticence, didn't answer, even though he knew the letters represented *Southlands* minus the vowels. Mr Pearson was in the middle of explaining this when the door burst open and Miss O'Neil, the Head of Year 7, swept into the room with a dishevelled looking boy in tow. Like Harry he had ginger hair and freckles, but his closely cropped crew cut and impish face meant that he looked far from angelic. He wore heavy, dark rimmed glasses and seemed to have troublemaker written all over him.

'This young man is Joe Robinson, who should be in your class, but decided he would rather be with his friends in 7N,' she informed Mr Pearson with annoyance and exasperation in her voice. She pointed to the chair next to Harry and ordered sternly, 'Sit there and take that smirk off your face!'

Joe sat down slowly and sullenly with a loud scraping of his chair. Harry glanced sideways and was amazed at Joe's brazen lack of concern as he was made to copy his timetable. Unlike the others, who had come with bulging new pencil cases, Joe hadn't even brought a pen. Harry promptly passed him one of his pens and Joe winked at him and said, 'Ta, mate'.

Catherine O'Neil had a formidable

reputation and was feared as much by other members of staff as by the pupils. She was unmarried and middle aged and colleagues called her *The Ice Queen* behind her back, because of her cold, unsympathetic character and imperious manner.

She turned to speak to Mr Pearson in low tones which Harry and Joe strained to overhear, catching only the odd words. Harry heard the words *troublemaker* and *miscreant* mentioned and it was clear that separating Joe from his old friends was a deliberate ploy.

'What's a miscreant, miss? Is that good?' Joe asked mischievously. She was taken aback by Joe's cheeky manner. Her mouth hung open and her eyebrows were raised in a stunned expression. She seemed momentarily at a loss for words.

Mr Pearson quickly stepped forward, leaned over Joe and said firmly, 'You shouldn't be listening to private conversations, Joe Robinson. Now get on with copying your timetable, without another word, or you'll be spending the whole of break with me.' Joe gave a slight turn of his head towards Harry, then a wink, before bending over his timetable and scribbling with mock urgency. The knowing wink and the twinkle in his eyes suggested that Joe knew very well the meaning of *miscreant*.

The Head of Year resumed her conversation in a low agitated voice that intrigued the two boys and invited further eavesdropping. They heard the words *admissions policy* and *should have refused* and drew their own conclusions.

When the bell sounded for break, Joe had to stay behind and Harry didn't see him again till near the end of break. Harry was talking to Poppy and Rachel when Joe came up to him.

''Ere ya can have ya pen back,' Joe said, thrusting the pen towards him.

'It's all right. You can keep it. You might need it.'

'Nah, I never carry a pen. It would ruin me street cred. You can be me pen holder.' Harry took the pen meekly and put it in his pocket. 'Did ya hear what old Frosty Knickers said about me?' Joe asked with a grin.

Poppy and Rachel giggled at this but Harry answered tactfully, 'Not really.'

'She must think 'cos I can't see too well

that I can't hear too well either. She more or less said that she doesn't want me at this school, but she doesn't scare me.' Harry didn't doubt it from what he had seen already.

It was now the end of break and pupils were heading back into school. 'See ya, later mate,' Joe said cheerfully as he moved off in the opposite direction to Harry.

'Maths is this way,' Harry pointed out, trying to be helpful.

Joe just grinned and whispered, 'But I'm goin' the scenic route.'

Chapter 2

When Joe arrived 10 minutes late for the maths lesson he gave the excuse that he had got lost. The teacher, Mrs Brierley, wasn't fooled by this and gave him a strong warning about being late. Joe didn't seem the least concerned and Harry was surprised when he chose to sit next to him again. The class had already started a maths assessment test and Joe was quickly given his sheet. Without saying a word, he put out his hand towards Harry and was given a pen. He winked a *thank you* and then swung back on his chair, nonchalantly studying the sheet and at the same time chewing the end of Harry's pen. Harry half expected him to announce that he couldn't do the work, but eventually Joe's chair came down with a bang and he started rattling off the answers. He finished before Harry or anyone else in the class and then started swinging again on his chair, his arms folded across his chest. Mrs Brierley pounced on him. 'Stop swinging on your chair and get on with your work!'

'Calm down my dear! I've finished,' Joe

said in a condescending voice.

Mrs Brierley's face flushed with anger. She picked up his sheet and quickly scanned his answers. The rest of the class had been distracted from their work and became engrossed in the unfolding drama. They now waited for the expected explosion, but it never arrived. Her expression changed to astonishment and she seemed satisfied with Joe's answers. Harry hadn't finished his sheet so she knew that he couldn't have copied his answers. 'Well, Joe, it looks like you're not as daft as you look!'

'Gee, thanks,' Joe grinned, pretending to be flattered by the backhanded compliment.

'Looks like I'll have to reward you with something harder to do.'

The cheeky grin disappeared and Joe scowled back at her. 'Er, no thanks I 'ave to give me brain a rest now.' With that he slumped down on the desk, his head resting on his folded arms. Mrs Brierley decided it was easier to just leave him and avoid further confrontation. After all he had finished his test and at least he was quiet, she told herself as the class resumed their work and peace was restored. Joe, however, was not prepared to give up the limelight so easily. Within a few minutes he began to snore loudly, sending ripples of laughter across the classroom.

Mrs Brierley had a face of thunder as she got up from her desk. She had to restrain her natural instinct to give him a clout across the head and shook him on the shoulder instead. Joe pretended to be woken from a deep sleep and straightened up suddenly with comic effect. Mrs Brierley was the only person not amused by Joe's antics. Her eyes bulged and tiny specs of spit flew out of her mouth as her voice rose to a high-pitched crescendo. 'Go and stand outside my classroom at once, you silly boy! I'll deal with you later!'

Joe wasn't intimidated by her outburst and began wiping his face and chest with his hand in exaggerated gestures. This caused further titters from those at the front who had witnessed the flying spit. He left the classroom with the self-satisfied grin of someone who had achieved what he had set out to do all along. The end of the lesson couldn't come soon enough for the teacher. She kept glancing at her watch and the thin glass panel in the door to see if Joe was making faces. It was only when she opened the door to let out the class that she realised why he hadn't made an encore. Joe was nowhere to be seen.

Harry and the rest of 7S could also see that he had absconded and as they headed for their next lesson, Joe was the only topic of conversation. 'Looks like your friend's done a runner,' Poppy remarked as they walked along the corridor.

'He's not really my friend. He just sat next to me,' Harry corrected her.

'He's totally hilarious isn't he? I've never laughed so much in a lesson before,' Poppy declared.

'Definitely not in a maths lesson, or come to think of it a maths test,' Rachel said laughingly. 'I would hate to be a teacher trying to teach someone like Joe. He must be every teacher's nightmare!'

'I agree but wasn't it amazing how quickly he finished his test?' Harry said.

'He must be a genius and yet he looks the opposite,' Poppy observed and then added thoughtfully, 'Let's hope the teacher takes the distractions into account when she marks our papers.'

The next lesson was English and Harry

was pleased when Mr Johnson acknowledged him with an extra big smile. He smiled back and noticed for the first time that Roddy's long hair was tied back in a ponytail. It must have been tucked under his cycle helmet when they met earlier. Roddy made an immediate impression on the girls in the class as they admired his ruggedly handsome features, his long hair and trendy clothes.

There were approving murmurs as they took their places and Harry overheard Poppy say, 'He's gorgeous! He looks like a singer in a rock band.'

The class were in a bubbly mood that Mr Johnson managed to harness to his advantage as he led the class in a lively discussion of ideas for a piece of creative writing. Joe had been conspicuous by his absence and, by the time he made an appearance, the class were already writing quietly. This time it was Mr Pearson who brought Joe to the class. He had been found loitering in the toilets and his excuse - that he had *the runs* – hadn't been believed. Joe, however, continued to act out the part, walking with his legs apart, like a toddler with a sticky nappy. He milked the situation for all it was worth as he eased his bottom onto the seat next to Harry. The class could not contain their laughter and even Mr Johnson had to suppress a smile.

However, the disruptive effect of Joe's antics prompted a furious reaction from Mr Pearson. The class saw a completely different side to their genial form teacher as he launched an angry tirade that instantly wiped the smiles from their faces. He was rarely moved to such anger and, like a dormant volcano that suddenly erupts, was all the more memorable for its intensity. When the hot lava had subsided the classroom landscape had changed completely. Even Joe was subdued and Mr Pearson was able to leave behind a still tableau of seemingly solidified figures bent over their work.

Roddy Johnson's classroom was situated next door to the dining hall and kitchens. The quietness in the classroom meant that every sound in the kitchen could be heard: the scraping of metal spoons, the clattering and clanging of pans and metal trays and the rattle and thump of baskets of cutlery as they were put into position. On top of all this the kitchen ladies called to each other in loud voices.

'Are those chips ready yet, Marjorie?'

'Can we have some more beans please?'

'Watch that tray's red hot!'

The non-food related snippets of conversation were the most entertaining.

'Did you get that new top you were after from Asda, Avril?'

'Yes.'

'Is she on the pull?' another voice asked.

This was followed by cackles of laughter and then even more when the reply came back from Avril, 'Not blinking likely at my age!'

The sounds of the kitchen were not the only distraction. The smell of sausages, meat pies and chips wafted ever stronger into the classroom, tantalising the taste buds of the hungry pupils. The hunger pangs that Joe was experiencing were more like starvation pangs, as it seemed like an eternity since he had eaten a cooked meal. He felt weak with hunger and his mouth was watering so much that he had to constantly swallow saliva. He found it difficult to concentrate on his work but forced himself to make the effort. Mr Johnson had warned the class that anyone who hadn't produced a satisfactory amount of work would be kept behind when the dinner bell sounded. He had been looking directly at Joe and the message had obviously got through to him. It was all the motivation Joe needed after he weighed up his chances of pushing past the teacher's tall, muscular frame. At his previous school he had not hesitated to barge past any female teacher who tried to detain him from his dinner.

Joe and Harry finished at about the same time and Mr Johnson came over to check their work. He praised both boys for their efforts but seemed especially pleased with Joe. 'Well done, Joe, I can't find a single spelling mistake and you've used punctuation and paragraphing correctly.'

Joe squirmed with embarrassment and said, 'It was easy, sir.' Then, emboldened by the praise, he asked cheekily, 'Does that mean I can be first out for me dinner?'

Mr Johnson hesitated before answering. He didn't want to appear weak, yet he knew that building a good rapport with Joe was the key to success with this class. He frowned and his eyes narrowed. 'I've not forgotten your late arrival or your foolery.'

'But I did make up for it; I worked really 'ard after Mr Pearson blew 'is top. I promise I won't mess around in ya lesson again. I was only showin' ya me actin' skills, sir.'

The teacher's face instantly brightened and a broad smile replaced the frown. 'Oh really? Well, in that case you should join the Drama Club. We need natural performers like you and you seem to know how to work an audience. You've certainly got the gift of the gab so that could be useful too.' As Joe absorbed what he had said and basked in the glow of unexpected praise, Mr Johnson turned his attention to the rest of the class. 'You can pack up now 7S. Mr Pearson will be pleased to hear that you all worked well in the end,' looking at Joe as he said this. Before he had finished saying, 'You can start lining up at the door,' Joe had darted forward and stood in front of the door. Harry wondered if that was the reason he chose to sit at the front. The other pupils began lining up behind Joe in the aisle. 'Wait for the bell before you go and no running!' Mr Johnson instructed them. 'And that reminds me, I'm so pleased that your affliction seems to have cleared up, Joe.'

Joe looked puzzled for a moment and then the penny dropped. 'Oh, ya mean the runs? I'm all right now.' Joe didn't mind the joke. Most teachers got on his nerves and he loved to wind them up; but he had already decided that Mr Johnson wasn't one of them.

As soon as the bell rang, Joe made a dash for the dining hall doors. He quickly grabbed a tray and cutlery and was the first to arrive at the serving hatch where three ladies wearing blue overalls and white caps were waiting. He tried to coax them into giving him extra food by telling them that he was starving and that he didn't get a cooked meal at home. The ladies felt sorry for him because he looked undernourished and they suspected he was telling the truth. He managed to earn himself a few extra chips and mushy peas, but the lady serving the meat pie, glancing at the supervisor, told him gruffly, 'Don't try it on with me, you greedy little beggar.' Despite the warning, she still gave him the largest portion she could find. Joe added a filling sponge pudding and a drink to his tray before handing in his free dinner ticket at the till. He quickly claimed the nearest table and couldn't eat his dinner fast enough. He ate from his tray and a white haired, blue overalled, dinner supervisor immediately approached.

'Could you put your tray back please!' Joe took no notice and continued to eat so she tried to explain, 'There's others that need to use that tray and it's taking up too much space.'

'In a minute, grandma. I'll sort it.'

Soon other pupils from 7S including Poppy and Rachel joined Joe at the table. Out of the corner of his eye, he saw Harry carrying a tray of food and he seemed uncertain whether to join his table. Joe beckoned him over and as Harry unloaded his tray, the supervisor still hovered. She repeated her request irritably, 'Are you going to take that tray back?'

'Yes, of course,' Harry replied politely, thinking she meant him. 'I'll take yours back too if you like, Joe.'

Harry walked off with the two trays and Joe called to the supervisor, 'I told ya I'd sort it grandma!'

She glared back at him with obvious displeasure and before moving away warned him, 'I'll be watching you!'

While Harry chatted to Poppy and Rachel and some boys from 7S, Joe was much more interested in what food was being left on their plates. His interest in food bordered on an obsession. His scavenging eyes became fixed on an uneaten sausage on one boy's plate and a half-eaten slice of Bakewell tart on Poppy's plate. He was disappointed when the Bakewell tart was eventually eaten, but when the sausage plate was pushed aside, he made his move. 'Ya leavin' that sausage?' he asked. When the boy nodded, Joe popped the end of the sausage in his mouth and held it like a greasy cigar. He pretended to puff on it and said in a heavy American accent, 'Now ya know why they call him the human dustbin!' The other pupils were amused but the clever tactic worked. From then onwards they always knew where to direct any unwanted food.

Harry and Joe hung around together for the rest of the lunch break and when Joe paid a visit to the boys' toilets, Harry followed him. He immediately regretted it. The smell of smoke hung heavily in the air and tell-tale spirals were drifting upwards from the furthest cubicle. Two older boys were loitering outside the cubicle apparently waiting for their friend to finish his cigarette. Harry almost stopped when he realised they were the same boys who had set upon him that morning. They looked up from examining a mobile phone, but it was Joe they recognised first.

'Hiya, Joe. Not seen ya in ages. Got any ciggies?'

'Nah. Gave 'em up.' He knew the boys but they weren't his friends.

'Who's this you've got 'ere?'

'E's me mate, 'Arry.'

'Really? I thought he was the Milky Bar Kid. No, I mean the Mars Bar Kid!' They both laughed and Joe guessed that they were the boys Harry had told him about.

'Did it really take two big lads like you to rob a Mars bar? It must 'ave bin a jumbo one. Did ya think it was a phone? I've always 'ad trouble diallin' out on a jumbo Mars bar. Can never get a signal,' Joe joked.

Harry looked on in horror as Joe took on two boys nearly twice his size, fighting them with words, rather than fists. He had given a hint of the jokes that could be spread about them and they knew how funny Joe could be when he started taking the mickey.

Harry was relieved when one of them merely replied, 'Ha, ha, you're so funny.'

'I know I am, but like I said 'Arry's me mate.' At last he turned away from them and Harry gave him a pleading look. He wanted to run away from there as fast as he could, but Joe wasn't in the same hurry. To his dismay, Joe said, 'I'll not be a mo,' and then disappeared into one of the cubicles. Harry was left standing awkwardly by the sinks with the two thugs a few feet away. He had completely lost the urge to pee so he busied himself washing his hands while waiting for Joe. He had never washed his hands so carefully nor dried them so thoroughly in his life and was thankful that the other two lost interest in him. One of them started calling to his friend to hurry up and finish his cigarette and they exchanged a few words. The other boy turned his attention to examining the mobile phone again. He seemed unfamiliar with it and Harry guessed it had been stolen.

A maelstrom of thoughts swirled through

Harry's mind and the worst of them became a reality when the headmaster chose that moment to march into the boys' toilets. He was wearing his black gown over his suit which added to his air of authority. Harry's urge to pee had suddenly returned, but Mr Atkinson wasn't interested in him. He prided himself on being able to spot a villain and Harry didn't fit the description. The other two did, and were well known to him.

'I thought I could smell smoke! Have you two been smoking in here?'

The two boys tried to look innocent and both said, 'No sir.'

'Well somebody certainly has!' he roared. 'Empty out your pockets and you two in the cubicles, get out here now!'

By the time Joe and the smoker emerged from their cubicles, the headmaster had taken a lighter, matches and a mobile phone from the other two.

'Well, well, Carl Watkins again! I might have known.' There was no mistaking the smell of smoke on his clothing and he too carried a lighter. Mr Atkinson needed no further evidence, not even the cigarette butt that Carl had failed to flush down the toilet.

With the triumphant look of a policeman who had caught criminals in the act, he now gave Joe a long, hard look. He was convinced he had found another smoker, as Joe seemed to match his profile of usual suspects.

'What's your name?'

'Joe Robinson, sir.'

'And what are you doing in here?'

'I've bin doin' a poo, sir,' Joe replied with such an honest, angelic face that the other boys had to bite their lips to stop themselves laughing.

Mr Atkinson didn't see the funny side at all and yelled at him, 'You've been smoking haven't you?'

'No sir.'

'Empty out your pockets!'

The contents of Joe's pockets provided another source of amusement for the other boys as he dragged out an unbelievable amount of unsavoury rubbish, but no smoking materials. Mr Atkinson was determined to find evidence of smoking and prove himself right. As he went to look in the cubicle Joe had occupied, Joe shouted out a warning, 'I'd be careful goin' in there with matches sir!'

This time the other boys, including Harry, couldn't contain their laughter and Mr Atkinson was absolutely furious. No one had ever dared to speak to him like that or try to make such a fool of him before. Desperately wanting to wipe the smile from Joe's face, he knew he had to remove him from the audience. 'I'll deal with the rest of you later.' He looked sternly at Joe and the voluminous wings of his gown billowed as he beckoned him to come forward. 'You, Joe Robinson, come with me now!' Joe was meant to follow him out of the toilets with his head bowed in shame. Instead, behind the headmaster's back, he flapped his arms like wings, in a final act of mockery.

Harry didn't see Joe again until afternoon registration when he returned from the headmaster's office brandishing a report card. He relayed to Mr Pearson and the rest of the class what the headmaster had said to him, announcing proudly that it was the first time Mr Atkinson had ever placed a pupil on report after only half a day at school.

'What did you say to that, Joe?'

'I said *Gee thanks*.'

Mr Pearson suspected that as far as Joe

was concerned, the report card wouldn't have the desired effect.

The afternoon lessons seemed to fly by unusually quickly for Harry. He was vaguely aware that it had something to do with the friendships he had formed with Poppy and Rachel but especially with Joe. Lessons were never dull with him around and he kept the class fully entertained. The boys were completely different and yet both felt an immediate connection, enjoying each other's company and the same sense of humour. Harry felt irresistibly drawn to Joe like a guilty pleasure that he knew deep down he should be resisting.

Chapter 3

Staythorpe House was a large, three storey, detached Victorian property which had been bought for a bargain price by Martin and Alice Cowper-Smyth during the property slump of the early 1990's. It was conveniently situated on Maybank Avenue, just a short drive from the offices of the law firm where they both worked. They saw the house as an ideal family home with 5 bedrooms, 2 reception rooms and a large dining kitchen at the heart of it. The rooms were elegant and spacious with high ceilings and original features which gave the house great character.

A local builder, Robert Jones, was employed by the couple to carry out some repairs and improvements when they moved into the house. Robert was about 40 years of age and was surprisingly scrawny for a builder. He had a gaunt face with a swarthy complexion and dark hair.

'Call me Bob,' he said cheerfully when they first met. 'I don't swear like a builder and I don't look like one, but at least I've got the right name!'

'*Bob the Builder* it is then,' Martin agreed with a grin. He liked Bob and he soon proved an excellent worker as he often worked late to finish fitting the new kitchen.

'My wife Vera would love a big kitchen like this,' he told them while screwing the door hinge on the last kitchen cabinet. 'She used to be a professional cook and she's always complaining that the kitchen in our flat isn't big enough to *swing a cat.*'

With his face stuck inside the cabinet, Bob couldn't see the smile that crossed Alice's face. She had always been amused by that old expression and was far too polite to ask, 'Who would want to *swing a cat* anyway?'

Before she could reply Bob explained, 'She worked at Besant's Bakery since leaving school and made all different kinds of cakes by hand. Then that big supermarket opened down the road and took away most of their trade. It was only a matter of time before the bakery had to close and Vera lost her job.'

'That's a shame,' Alice replied sympathetically. 'Has she been able to find any other work?'

'No, not yet. It's difficult finding anything these days. She's not a good traveller. Buses make her sick, and she can't drive. The bakery suited her down to the ground because she could walk to work.'

As Bob started putting away his tools, Martin and Alice exchanged meaningful glances. They had both thought of the ideal solution.

'Bob, do you think Vera would like to work here as a sort of housekeeper?' Alice asked tentatively. 'It would involve cleaning and perhaps preparing the odd evening meal. Martin and I have already discussed advertising for a cleaner. With working full time, I don't get the chance to do much cleaning and cooking so it would be a big help to me.'

Bob looked both surprised and pleased. 'Obviously you would have to speak to Vera about it, but it sounds ideal for her as it's only a ten-minute walk from our flat. She would love cooking in a kitchen like this and she's one of the few women I know who actually enjoys cleaning; she even likes ironing, but don't tell her I said that!'

'But are you sure it won't be too much for her?' Alice asked.

'Oh no. She likes to keep busy and I certainly prefer it. Stops her being bored and thinking too much!'

Alice laughed at this, 'Oh dear. I better not tell her you said that either!'

The following evening Bob introduced his wife Vera to the couple and she was given a tour of the house. Two years younger than her husband, she was small with short wiry black hair, round shoulders and a large double chin that wobbled when she spoke. She had the same warm-hearted nature as her husband and, as Bob had predicted, she accepted the offer of work without hesitation and marvelled at the huge kitchen.

'I've always wanted a kitchen like this,' she said looking around her and unaware of the 'told you so' smile on Bob's face. 'Would you mind if I baked a few cakes and a nice pudding as well?'

Martin screwed up his face and made a pretence of considering the proposal. Then he declared with a wink, 'I think we could put up with that! When can you start?'

Vera started work the very next day and

it didn't take long for the couple to realise what a treasure they had found as Vera ensured the smooth running of the household. Even after Harry had been born and Alice gave up work, she continued to work for the family.

Martin and Alice had bought Staythorpe House on the assumption that they would have a large family. Unfortunately when Harry was only a week old, the couple were given the devastating news that there could be no more babies. Both parents were bitterly disappointed. Alice was already feeling unwell after a difficult birth and her 'baby blues' deepened into an overwhelming sadness. With no relatives living nearby to give help on a daily basis, she came to rely more and more on Vera's help.

'I've not been able to have any children of my own,' Vera confided in her one day, 'so I'm only too pleased to look after the little 'un.'

'Oh, I'm sorry. I didn't know. It must have been much worse for you. At least we've got Harry.'

'Yes, you have to be thankful for that,' Vera told her, hoping to put things into perspective.

Vera took on the role of part time nanny and, as soon as he could talk, Harry called her Nan. The name had stuck ever since.

Martin coped with the disappointment of not having more children by concentrating on his career with even more commitment. As well as his legal work he became increasingly involved in politics and his wife fully supported him in his ambition to become a Member of Parliament. Harry was 7 years old when the Labour Party won the General Election and his father was finally elected M.P. Harry's life changed completely as he began to see less of his parents. Martin rented a flat in London where he stayed when attending Parliament and even when he came home he was often preoccupied with constituency business. Alice began to work for her husband and stayed more and more in the flat in London. The couple had little time to devote to their son, but at least they knew he was well looked after by Nan and Bob. It was a very convenient arrangement for the Cowper-Smyths.

'Too convenient,' Nan muttered to her husband, as they settled down for the night in the bedroom now permanently allocated for them. 'I sometimes wonder whether we've made it too convenient for them to spend time away from Harry. They're so wrapped up in themselves and their careers that they seem to forget that they still have a son. It's not Harry's fault he doesn't have any brothers or sisters, but he keeps thinking that he's the one who's disappointed them,' Nan continued, with passion in her voice.

Bob knew that it was pointless trying to stop her when she was in full flow, so he just repeated, 'I know love, I know.'

'I just feel so sorry for him. He's always been such a solitary little boy, rattling around in this big house on his own.'

'Well, he'll always get plenty of love from us and that makes up for anything else. Now you need to switch off your mind from this or you'll never get to sleep.' As he lay down, trying to get to sleep, Bob had to admit that they seemed to be spending almost as much time at Staythorpe House as they did at their own flat.

Having formed such a close bond with the boy, Nan and Bob were naturally very upset when Martin and Alice decided to send Harry to a boarding school at the age of 9. 'We think it will be the making of him,' Martin tried to explain to them. 'He hasn't made any friends at his present school and the teachers have told us he's a bit of a loner.'

'We're hoping that boarding school will give him the companionship of children his own age and encourage him to make friends,' Alice added. They didn't mention that they were concerned that Harry spent so much time on his own or in the company of much older people like Nan and Bob.

'Has Harry agreed to go?' Nan asked.

'Yes.'

Nan guessed that Harry, ever eager to please, had hidden his true feelings. She had to fight back the tears when he left and was haunted for days by the sorrowful, pleading look Harry gave her from the car window as he was driven away. It broke her heart when Harry confided in her, after one term, how much he wanted to stay at home. After two years at boarding school, Harry's parents finally realised how desperately unhappy Harry was and how much he wanted to attend a local comprehensive instead. Nan had dropped a hint to Harry's parents when he seemed more withdrawn and introverted. She didn't trust herself to say more as she was worried what words might come tumbling out if she said too much.

Nan had plenty to say in private when she found out that both Martin and Alice would be attending a European convention in the same week that Harry started at Southlands School. 'They should be here with him on his first day, not swanning about in Brussels. I hope they don't think that a ten-minute phone call makes up for it - or all those expensive presents in his bedroom. The one thing lacking is the most precious gift of all – their time!'

'I know love, I know. You've said it before,' Bob tried to calm her. Then he said brightly, 'I see you've had a good baking session.'

'Well, he deserves a bit of spoiling.'

'Here's me thinking you'd made these cakes for me.' His hand hovered over the chocolate éclairs and, despite her playful slap, he managed to grab and devour one in a matter of seconds. Bob's favourite pastime was testing Nan's cakes and pastries, yet he remained surprisingly thin.

Nan said he burnt off the calories because he could never sit still for long. She envied his metabolism because she only had to look at a cake to put on weight. She was plump, rather than fat, and Harry just thought of her as cuddly.

By the time Harry started his new school life at Southlands, Nan and Bob had worked for the family for almost 15 years. They had both aged in that time, but Harry could only remember them as they were now. They had always been there for him, throughout his life. Something he couldn't say about his own parents who were becoming a more distant presence.

As he neared home after his first day at school, Harry could picture the scene in his mind. Nan and Bob would be waiting to greet him, eager to hear about his day and she would probably have baked some cakes and cooked him his favourite tea. When he opened the front door, the mouth-watering aromas confirmed that he had guessed correctly. Harry got a welcoming smile from Bob and a great big hug from Nan. She whispered soothingly in his ear, 'Hope you never get too big for one of your Nan's hugs.'

'Never,' Harry replied positively.

'Now tell us about your day!' Nan urged, even though from his body language and good spirits, she already knew the answer.

They sat around the kitchen table while Harry gave them a carefully edited version of what had happened that day. There was no mention of the attack on the way to school or the trouble Joe had caused. He told them about his new friends Poppy, Rachel and Joe Robinson who had ginger hair and freckles like him and made everyone in the class laugh. 'He's really funny but he's also very clever,' Harry enthused. 'He always finds the work easy and finishes before me.'

Nan and Bob exchanged glances and seemed pleased. They had never heard Harry speak so enthusiastically about school before.

'His hair's a brighter shade of ginger than mine, but it's cut really short in a crew cut. You hardly noticed he was ginger with his hair cut so short. Joe's a lot tougher than me so I didn't get any name calling while he was around.'

Nan had guessed where this was leading so she quickly interrupted him, 'Don't even think about it my lad. Your mother would have a fit!'

'You would look like a right pair of twins,' Bob added.

Harry smiled back at them. 'I didn't say I wanted a crew cut. Anyway we wouldn't look alike 'cos he's got glasses.'

Harry spoke on the phone to his parents that night for longer than he had ever done before. He told them about Poppy and Rachel and described Joe with the same enthusiasm and careful editing as before. His parents noticed the exuberance in his voice and were amazed at the difference in him. They were very pleased that Harry seemed to like the school and had found new friends at last. They wanted to encourage the friendships and told Harry that he could invite them to the house whenever he liked. Alice spoke to Nan afterwards and Harry heard Nan say, 'I know, we thought the same.'

Harry wondered what they would think if they knew what Joe was really like – a cross between *Dennis the Menace* and *Horrid Henry*.

Chapter 4

The next morning Harry set off for school without the apprehension he had felt the previous day. The walk to school was brisk and uneventful but when he arrived in the form room Joe wasn't there and he was marked absent on the register. Harry didn't have much time to miss Joe because he was soon drawn into conversation.

'Do you know if Joe is coming to school today?' Poppy asked.

Harry shrugged his shoulders, 'I've no idea. I don't think Joe's got a phone so I can't call him to find out.'

'Well, it's double PE first lesson and I've heard the PE staff are really strict, especially about things like punctuality. Apparently anyone who arrives late has to take a cool shower as a punishment. The more times you are late, the colder the shower,' Rachel informed them.

'It sounds awful,' Poppy said. 'We better make sure we're not late. It's a pity we couldn't warn Joe in case he comes in late like yesterday. He would be better off missing the lesson altogether.'

Rachel looked at her friend and a huge grin started to spread across her face, as if something had just dawned on her. 'You've got a bit of a soft spot for Joe, haven't you, Pops?'

Poppy blushed and hotly denied it. 'No! I haven't!'

'Oh yes you have! And I think Joe likes you too. I've seen the way he keeps looking across at you when he's done something funny. He always checks to see if you're smiling.'

'No he doesn't!' Poppy said, even though she knew it was true.

Rachel diplomatically backed down, sensing that the teasing was annoying her friend. 'Soz, Pops. I was only kiddin'.' The expression on Harry's face told her that he didn't like teasing either; it brought back too many painful memories.

Trying to change the subject, Poppy turned her attention to her favourite gripe. 'I wish they would let us girls play football along with the boys. It's horrible playing netball with sissy girls who can't even throw or catch a ball and squeal when they drop it!'

Rachel rolled her eyes. 'We've had all

this at our last school,' she explained to Harry. 'Poppy was better at football than a lot of the boys and would have played for the school team if she was a boy.'

'She would definitely be better than me. I like watching sport but I'm not much use taking part,' Harry admitted.

Soon afterwards the bell for the first lesson sounded. 7S pupils headed out of the main entrance and then broke into a disorderly gallop around the outside of the school to the sports centre.

'Come on, Harry! We don't want to be last,' Poppy shouted. They shared this lesson with 7T who had managed to arrive a minute before them, since their form room was nearer.

Waiting in the entrance to the sports centre were two scowling, track suited figures. Both had a whistle dangling from a ribbon around their necks and had a clipboard in their hands. The smaller figure was Miss Watts who quickly marshalled the girls into their changing area. She was dwarfed by Mr McMullen, Head of P.E, a giant of a man with a thick neck, muscular arms and chest and huge hands and feet. His flabby beer belly added to his bulk. His face bore the scars of a former rugby player with misshapen, cauliflower ears and a broken nose. Although he looked like a man in his late 40's, he had the hair of a much younger man. It didn't take long for the boys to notice that there was something unnatural about his hair. The hair on top didn't match the sides and back, fuelling speculation that he was wearing a toupee. Mr McMullen's crowning glory became an object of intense fascination and discreet scrutiny. However, for the moment the boys had to keep their thoughts to themselves as their names were ticked on the clipboard.

By the time Harry reached the boys' changing area most of the 7T boys had already changed into their P.E. kit. Two of them began staring and pointing at Harry and called out, 'Hey ginger nut!'

Harry ignored them and carried on getting changed, but when they repeated the same chant he could feel his face flush with embarrassment. Suddenly Harry heard a familiar voice singing behind him, 'Yes, we're the ginger nutters, the ginger, ginger nutters. Dada, da, da, dada, da, da.' Joe accompanied this with a comical dance that brought smiles to the faces of everyone in the room, even the two boys in 7T who had started it.

'Sorry lads, ya can't be in our gang. Only gingers in the ginger nutters,' he told them proudly before continuing his song and dance. 'Yes, we're the ginger nutters, the ginger, ginger nutters. Dada, da, da...'

At that moment the door to the changing room was flung open and Mr McMullen marched in, bellowing, 'What on earth do you think you are doing?' He pointed at Joe, whose head was now tilted upwards, staring open mouthed at the massive Goliath towering over him. The room had fallen ominously silent and even Joe didn't dare give the obvious answer.

'What's your name?'

'Joe Robinson.'

'It's *sir* when you speak to me. I'll try again. What's your name?'

'Sir Joe Robinson.' Joe said this so innocuously that Mr McMullen was left floundering in exasperation.

'You stupid boy! You should say *Joe Robinson, sir*. Don't think you can make a fool out of me!' he warned menacingly. Some of the boys had to turn away with their hands over their mouths, trying to suppress their sniggers. Ever the consummate actor, Joe kept his face straight as if he had no idea why the teacher was so annoyed. Mr McMullen checked his clipboard. 'And why haven't you been marked on the register?'

'Sir, I came in the wrong entrance..... sir.' Joe had in fact sneaked into the sports centre through a service entrance hoping to find some spare P.E. kit in a lost property cupboard. He had only stopped his search when he heard the 7T boys chanting.

'Well, make sure you come in the <u>right</u> entrance next time! And why haven't you changed into your P.E kit, you miserable little boy?'

'Sir, I don't 'ave any P.E. kit..... sir.'

'What? No P.E. kit!' Mr McMullen cried in disbelief.

'Sir, it got nicked, sir,' Joe added lamely.

'Don't try that on with me! I don't believe you and I won't take that as an excuse. I presume you don't have a medical note?'

Joe shook his head.

Mr McMullen was losing patience and wanted to conclude the conversation that had captured the attention of all the other boys and held up his lesson. He laid down the rules unequivocally. 'Let me make this clear to Joe and all the rest of you. We do NOT allow ANY slackers or smart AR...ticles in the P.E. Department.' He paused while his eyes rested on Joe, then he continued, 'Anyone who arrives unacceptably late to my lesson gets a cold shower. Anyone who forgets his P.E. kit gets lost property kit of my choosing. No one is excused P.E. without a medical note from a parent or guardian and anyone who even thinks of forging a note will live to regret it. My colleague, Mr Bell, is in the gym preparing some equipment for you so we better not keep him waiting any longer. Robinson, you come with me.'

The other boys trooped out and Joe followed Mr McMullen to the only storeroom he hadn't tried to open earlier. The teacher rummaged through a large cardboard box of clothing and found a pair of black football shorts that were obviously far too big for Joe and then a smile crossed his face as he produced an extra large Liverpool football shirt. He used this shirt as a punishment as boys from this area of

Manchester hated wearing it.

To his frustration Joe seemed positively delighted and exclaimed, 'Ah, sir, thanks! Me favourite team. Thanks, sir!'

Mr McMullen's face hardened as he handed over an ancient pair of pumps, usually worn in junior schools and a pair of odd socks. He couldn't understand why Joe wasn't bothered at all by the ridiculously baggy clothing. Any other boy would have been mortified and would have protested loudly and got changed slowly. But Joe wasn't like any other boy; he got changed quickly and cheerfully and he remained in good spirits even when some of the class laughed at his funny appearance. Joe loved being the centre of attention and the comical clothes gave him the perfect opportunity to play the class clown. When the teachers weren't looking he tried out a Charlie Chaplin walk or pulled out the waistband of his shorts and stuck out his tummy like a man with a huge beer belly. Later on he pretended to search frantically for something he had lost down his shorts. It looked hilariously funny because his shorts were so large and hung below his knees. Joe always timed his actions with split second accuracy so the teachers never managed to catch him in the act, even if they suspected something was going on. Mr Bell was a newly qualified teacher who was easily fooled and even the sharp eyed Mr McMullen couldn't watch Joe every minute of the lesson.

The boys were dispersed across the gym on various pieces of equipment – vaulting over the horse, climbing up ropes, running along upturned benches and rolling on mats. Joe showed great agility and balance despite being hampered by shorts that were in constant danger of falling down. He struggled much more with the exercises requiring upper body strength. Mr McMullen made sure he did extra press-ups and sit-ups as he was determined to punish Joe one way or another. At the end of the lesson Joe was ordered to put away the mats, benches and smaller equipment under the supervision of Mr Bell. Another boy was needed to help so Harry volunteered immediately. It was the first opportunity he had to thank Joe for helping with the bullies.

Joe just winked at him and chirped, 'That's all right, mate. We ginger nutters 'ave to stick together.' Then he continued more seriously, 'Listen 'Arry, I learned the 'ard way a long time ago; ya 'ave to put on a bit of an act with bullies. They get their kicks out of pickin' on people who're different, or weaker or on their own. If they call ya names, laugh about it as if ya don't care. I usually say *ginger nuts are me favourite biscuit too*, or somethin' like that. Don't let um see that they've got through to ya. If ya take away the satisfaction they get from hurtin' ya and seein' ya upset, they're more likely to leave ya alone. It can work sometimes with teachers too.'

Joe told Harry how deflated Mr McMullen looked when he told him Liverpool was his favourite team.

'So you're not really a Liverpool fan?'

'Of course I am. Wayne Rooney's me favourite player.' Harry looked puzzled for a moment before Joe admitted, 'I'm only kiddin'. It's definitely *not* Wayne Rooney. Steven Gerrard's me favourite player. Me dad's from Liverpool and we're all big Liverpool fans, but to be honest the way they've bin playin' lately it's no wonder me dad's bin depressed!' Both boys laughed at this and drew the attention of Mr Bell.

'Watch out! Young Tinga Ling's comin' over!' Joe warned.

'Less of the chattering lads and the sooner we'll get this job done!' Mr Bell called to them as he approached. 'Come on, I'll give you a hand.'

Neither boy spoke as Mr Bell helped them put away the last of the equipment and then hurried them to the changing room. Harry's mind was fully occupied trying to fathom the complex character of his new friend. On the one hand Joe was forever joking and yet there was another side to him that Harry glimpsed when he gave wise advice about bullying.

Joe's mind was also fully occupied thinking about the punishment Mr McMullen might have in store for him for being late. He could fool others easily enough, but he couldn't fool himself. He didn't know if he could be brave enough to follow the advice he had given to Harry. He wondered whether the rumours might have been exaggerated but that faint hope was soon dashed when he saw Mr McMullen waiting for him, his hands on his hips and a self-satisfied smirk on his face.

Mr McMullen didn't know Harry's name

so he jerked a thumb in the direction of the showers and said, 'You lad, get in that shower as fast as you can!' Joe moved forward to follow Harry but Mr McMullen's arm barred his way. 'Nice try, but not so fast Robinson. You don't think I've forgotten that you were late for my lesson, do you?'

Joe gave a wry smile, 'No sir.'

By this time the other boys in the changing room had stopped what they were doing and were straining to get a better view. There were few things they liked better than seeing someone else getting a good *telling-off*.

Mr McMullen was well aware of his audience and the air of hushed expectancy in the changing room. Relishing the opportunity to make an example of Joe once again, he leaned forward with his face so uncomfortably close that Joe felt his breath in hot waves. His warning was delivered slowly and deliberately. 'Don't you ever arrive late to my lesson again. Do you hear me?'

'No sir, I mean, yes sir,' Joe replied in meek confusion.

The teacher's eyes narrowed as he tried

to work out whether Joe was being deliberately stupid. He decided that no boy would ever provoke him in that way. 'You stupid, snivelling, pathetic little specimen! Get your kit off and I'll teach you a lesson you'll never forget!'

While Joe undressed, Mr McMullen selected the smallest key from his bunch and used it to unlock the plastic cover on the temperature controls for the showers. The controls were rarely adjusted and were kept locked and out of reach to prevent pupil misuse. Mr McMullen pushed the lever from midway in the red section to the furthest end of the blue section. He stepped back with evident satisfaction and turned his attention back to Joe who was now waiting, completely naked, at the entrance to the showers. Mr McMullen towered over Joe and could hardly disguise his sadistic pleasure in bullying such a small, skinny, insignificant boy. He shoved Joe towards the shower and said roughly, 'Don't come out till I tell you!'

The shower was still steamy when Joe stepped into it, but the momentary spluttering of the water supply was followed by the sudden surge of cold water.

Joe instinctively stepped back, away from the icy flow, but Mr McMullen's voice immediately bellowed, 'Robinson, get under that shower now!'

'Yes sir, I'm just gettin' some soap.' Joe had to shout so that he could be heard above the sound of the water. He bent down to pick up a remnant of soap from the gutter. He still got sprayed with cold water but he avoided the full force of the water for a few more seconds. Realising that it would give his body more time to adjust to the temperature, he deliberately let the soap slip out of his hands. It shot further down the gutter and he made a comical run after it, causing hoots of laughter from the onlookers.

'I'm warning you Robinson. Get under that water now!'

'Sorry sir, I can't see so well without me glasses and this soap keeps slippin' out of me 'and.'

'Robinson!'

Joe could delay no longer and although he tried to brace himself, the impact of the icy water almost took his breath away. His back was turned so at least Mr McMullen couldn't see the shock on his face. Joe braved the cold in the same way as a swimmer plunging into the sea in winter. He kept himself moving by vigorously rubbing the soap along his arms and legs and announced in a loud, chirpy voice, 'That's the trouble with cold water sir, ya don't get such a good lather!'

Mr McMullen was no doubt disappointed to see Joe take his shower with such calm indifference, as if he was used to taking a cool shower every day. He was gutted to hear Joe say, 'Sir, it's not so bad when ya get used to it. It's a good job I don't seem to feel the cold.'

Soon afterwards Mr McMullen told Joe he could get out of the shower. Joe's spirit remained unbroken as he dried himself with Harry's semi-damp towel. He chatted amiably to Mr McMullen who was standing near him.

'Sir, 'ave ya ever read a book called *A Kestrel for a Knave*?'

'No, I never read books.'

'There's a teacher in it who's a lot like you.'

'You mean strict?'

'Definitely, sir.'

Mr McMullen eventually lost interest in

Joe and wandered off.

Harry whispered, 'Joe Robinson, you never cease to amaze me. What was the shower really like?'

'What d'ya think? Blinkin' freezin'! I don't know how I stopped me teeth from chatterin'. But I wasn't goin' to let 'im know that.'

'You were very convincing, but you took a chance mentioning a teacher like him in *A Kestrel for a Knave*. He might remember that he was a bully in the film.'

'I'm not bothered. *Kes* is an old film. Anyway, all P.E. teachers are as thick as two short planks. Did ya see 'is face? He thought I was flatterin' 'im about being a strict teacher,' Joe chuckled. 'Watch this space, 'Arry. I'll get me own back on 'im one day.'

Chapter 5

The lunchtime supervisor watched eagle eyed as Joe, Harry, Poppy and Rachel threaded their way through the crowded dining hall, carrying their trays of food and finally finding a table where they could all sit together. She saw Harry, in his gentlemanly way, take the stack of trays back for the others.

'Thanks, Harry,' Poppy and Rachel called after him, but Joe was too busy eating to notice Harry or the supervisor who had marched across to him.

'I hope you're not making that other boy take your tray back.'

'Of course not, grandma. 'Arry's me mate and he offered. E's like that.' Joe replied cheerfully.

Poppy and Rachel looked at each other and Poppy confirmed, 'He did offer. He wasn't being bullied if that's what you're thinking.'

Ignoring Poppy and looking pointedly at Joe she said, 'Well he's not your slave so make sure you clear your own plates when you've finished.'

'All right, grandma. I will.'

Harry returned to the table at that moment. The supervisor was clearly annoyed with Joe and her ill fitting dentures wobbled and nearly dropped from her mouth as she snapped at him, 'Stop calling me grandma! I'm not your grandma, thank goodness!'

Joe couldn't resist telling her, 'Ya want to watch ya don't lose those falsies. They might drop into someone's dinner.' She turned away, pretending not to hear, to stop herself from throttling him.

Some of the other pupils were laughing but Poppy and Rachel felt sorry for the dinner lady and gave Joe a disapproving look. Harry certainly wasn't laughing and he turned on Joe. 'That wasn't funny. No wonder she looked upset. How would you like it if that lady really was your grandma and someone embarrassed her like that?' Harry surprised himself with his scathing outburst, but Joe just shrugged off the criticism as if he was well used to it.

'I don't have any grandmas.'

'Well, that's bad luck. I have three and they are all very nice.'

'Three! 'Ow did ya manage that?'

'One of them isn't my real grandma but I still call her Nan. She bakes the best cakes in the world and looks after me like a real grandma. You should come and meet her some time and you would know what I mean.'

Now Joe was interested. 'I would definitely like to meet 'er. When did ya say I could come?'

'What about tomorrow? I'll check with my parents and Nan but I'm sure they won't mind.'

Joe began to see Harry in a new light; he wasn't such a lapdog after all, more like a bulldog at times. Unlike the rougher, tougher, dim-witted friends Joe usually chose, Harry didn't egg him on and encourage him to overstep the mark. He didn't approve of everything Joe said or did and wasn't afraid to tell him so. Despite this, Joe never felt that Harry looked down on him. Instead he sensed that Harry looked up to him and that he could rely on his unswerving loyalty. On top of all that he had a Nan who made the best cakes in the world.

Whether it was Harry's influence, or the realisation that the dinner supervisor might ruin his chances with the other dinner ladies, Joe decided to make amends. The dinner supervisor was watching to make sure they cleared their table when they had finished. Joe approached her with his hands full of dirty dishes and his face full of contrition. 'Sorry about before, I was just 'avin' a bit of fun.' Joe had a great streak of mischief running all the way through him like a stick of rock, but he obviously wasn't all bad. The dinner supervisor just smiled back at him…. very carefully.

The two boys were full of childish excitement as they walked back to Harry's house the following day. Joe had never been invited to tea at anyone's house before and it was the first time Harry had brought home a friend. Harry's excitement was tempered by the secret fear that this new experience for both of them wouldn't live up to Joe's expectations. He asked Joe again, 'Are you sure your dad knows where you are and has given permission?'

'For the umpteenth time, stop worryin'! 'E knows and 'e's O.K about it.'

'Good. Nan would have kittens if they sent out search parties for you.'

Joe was very impressed when they arrived outside Staythorpe House and asked, 'Which part d'ya live in?'

'All of it,' Harry replied sheepishly.

Joe was gobsmacked as he had assumed the house was a block of three flats. His eyes were wide open and full of wonder as they stepped into the Victorian tiled hall. They were immediately met by the wonderful smell of home baking which Harry was well used to but caused Joe to spontaneously lick his lips.

Nan bustled towards them from the kitchen followed by Bob. She had been given strict instructions not to hug Harry in front of Joe and there was an awkward moment when she nearly forgot herself. Joe was made to feel very welcome and soon they were happily seated around the kitchen table with a drink and the first round of cake testing. Joe was on his best behaviour and, to Harry's relief, he refrained from singing *Bob the Builder* and staring at Nan's wobbly chin. After wolfing down a chocolate éclair and a slice of apple pie, he declared gallantly, ''Arry was right about ya cakes. They really are the best in the world!' Harry didn't need to say anything;

he beamed his thanks to Nan.

'You can test another batch after tea if you like, but I wouldn't want to spoil your appetite right now. Tea will be ready in about an hour and a half. Perhaps Joe might like to see your bedroom,' Nan suggested as she started to clear the plates.

Harry hadn't offered to show Joe the rest of the house in case he thought he was showing off. But as they walked through the hall again Joe said admiringly, 'I can't believe ya live in a place like this. It's like a mansion I've read about in books.' He popped his head round the half open door of the main lounge and asked, 'Are all the rooms like this?'

Harry just shrugged his shoulders. He didn't want to tell Joe that all the rooms were just as beautifully and expensively furnished. Instead he said, 'I'll show you a room you'll really like.'

Joe followed Harry up the stairs to the first landing where he was bewildered by the number of doors, even after Harry named them all. He pointed out the family bathroom, his parent's bedroom, the bedroom used by Nan and Bob when they stayed and another guest bedroom.

'That's my bedroom, the second on the right. I'll show you it later. Come on, there's another flight of stairs up here.' He led Joe up to a smaller third floor landing with fewer doors leading off. There was another guest bedroom and a smaller bathroom but Harry didn't bother naming them. He crossed the landing, through an archway and a short passageway to arrive at yet another door.

Joe had no idea what to expect. He had loved tagging along behind Harry, running up stairs and exploring the old house that represented a completely different world to the one he knew. He followed Harry into the room and let out a massive, 'Wow!' His head swivelled round to take in the magnificent 30ft oak-panelled snooker room. He hardly noticed the leather armchairs and settee or the beautiful period fireplace. His eyes were drawn to the full size snooker table dominating the middle of the room. A long canopy light was suspended overhead while a rack of cues and a scoreboard conveniently hung from the nearest wall.

Harry pulled back the dust cover to reveal the green baize cloth, randomly scattered with red and coloured balls from an abandoned game. Joe had never seen a full sized snooker table before and he marvelled at its sheer size. Harry could see the eagerness on his face as he asked, 'Are ya allowed to play on it?'

'Yes, but I never do. It's not much fun on your own. We can have a game if you like.'

Joe jumped at the chance. 'Fantastic! I've watched snooker on the telly and I've always wanted to have a go. The table doesn't look as big as this on the telly though.'

'It's not as easy as they make it look on telly either,' Harry reminded him as he selected a couple of the smallest cues. 'I can show you all I know, but that won't take long!' he joked. They practised potting balls without much success to begin with, but they helped each other work out angles and cueing techniques and gradually improved. They celebrated every ball they potted with fist clenching jubilation. Harry was pleased to see Joe enjoying himself so much. 'I thought you'd like this room. Dad says it was a gentlemen's den. They used to come here to get away from the ladies, smoke their cigars and have a drink, as well as play snooker. There's a darts board at the far end too.'

'Not bad eh! I bet the ladies didn't see much of um once they came up 'ere.'

They were still playing snooker, and Harry hadn't even shown Joe his bedroom, when Bob called them for their tea. They tucked into a delicious meal of succulent chicken, roast potatoes and sweet potatoes, broccoli, carrots, baby sweet corn and mangetout. For Joe the meal was a memorable experience. He had never enjoyed food as much in his life. He wasn't used to such an array of vegetables and some of them he had never tasted before. As they ate their meal together, Joe, with disarming honesty, told them that he felt like a fish out of water in Harry's home and that his council house, on a tough estate, was nothing like Staythorpe House.

'That doesn't matter!' Harry reassured him.

'Of course not,' Nan confirmed, but her female curiosity had been aroused. She had noticed that Joe's school uniform looked handed down and prompted her to ask casually, 'Do you have any brothers or sisters, Joe?'

'Yes, I've got three brothers and two sisters, but we don't all 'ave the same dad. I never really see um now 'cos I live with me dad and they live with me mum. Me mum and dad split up the day before me ninth birthday. She took the other kids with 'er but she didn't take me. I think 'er new partner said five kids was enough and they couldn't cope with any more boys. I was the youngest so maybe I was too much work for 'er. I took it badly at the time and started gettin' into trouble at school.'

Nan looked shocked. She hadn't expected to open up old wounds. 'I'm so sorry, Joe. I can imagine how you must have felt.' She didn't like to ask any more questions, but once started, Joe was unstoppable. He wanted to carry on and tell them the rest of the story, as if the unburdening of it was somehow helpful to him.

'She only lives a few miles away in Bolton but I never see 'er. She sends me big brother with bags of clothin' for me but doesn't come 'erself. I don't want to see 'er either 'cos of what she did to me dad. 'E went to pieces when she left and 'e had so many days off sick 'e lost his job. 'E's only left the house once in three years. 'E thinks people are laughin' at 'im or callin' 'im a lazy layabout. 'E 'as good days and bad days and on 'is bad days 'e can't even get out of bed. Each time 'e has a couple of good days, I think 'e's gettin' better, and then 'e slips back again.'

'It sounds like he's had a breakdown and is suffering from depression. He needs to get medical help for this,' Nan urged with concern in her voice.

'That's the problem. 'E won't see a doctor or nurse 'cos 'e thinks they'll take me away from 'im. I know I can look after 'im. I get cash from a machine to do the shoppin' and I do all the cookin' and washin'. I only do things like beans on toast or sausages and chips. Nothin' like this kind of food.' Joe didn't tell them that he would resort to stealing food from shops when the money ran out.

'Do you mean to say that you've been looking after your father on your own since your mum left?' Joe nodded and Nan continued, 'I don't think a boy of your age should be doing that. Don't you have any other relatives who could help?'

'I only 'ave one – me grandad, me dad's dad, but 'e lives in Stockport and 'as to catch two buses to get 'ere. 'E comes whenever 'e can and helps with a bit of cleanin' and fills in forms and things like that. 'E went with dad the only time 'e left the 'ouse and that was for a medical assessment so 'e could claim benefits. 'E got in a right state over that. Grandad said 'e was so panicky 'e couldn't breathe properly. Some people say that me dad's a lazy benefits scrounger or a thicko, but I know none of that's true. Before mum left 'im 'e had a job and worked 'ard. 'E's not thick either. 'E's read lots of books. People don't understand enough about depression. They think all 'e needs is a kick up the backside to pull 'imself together, but I know it's not as simple as that. Dad says it's all too easy to put labels on people and ya should never judge a book by its cover.'

'Well, that's certainly true!' Nan agreed with feeling. She felt guilty that she had misjudged Joe from his outward appearance, before she got to know him. Her first impression was to see Joe as a little scallywag, with too many rough edges to become a suitable friend for a gentle boy like Harry. How her opinion had changed! Like the others, she had listened spellbound as Joe told his story. He told it in a matter of fact way, without a trace of self-pity. She was filled with admiration for his loyalty to his father and his irrepressible spirit that meant he never let anything get him down. He remained cheerful, despite everything, and that cheerfulness rubbed off on others, including Harry. No wonder his father wanted to hold onto him. Joe had completely won her over and she even asked him to call her Nan.

Bob must have been thinking the same as Nan. He had remained silent during the meal, but now he was moved to speak seriously. 'Joe, I think you are a truly amazing boy, wise beyond your years, but you really shouldn't be dealing with things like this on your own at your age. When I take you home, I'd like to speak to your dad about getting help for both of you, without you being taken away. Looking after your dad must surely be affecting your school work, and I know he wouldn't want that.'

Joe didn't know what to say as he wasn't sure how his father would react to interference and he didn't like to say so.

It was Harry who came to Joe's rescue by suggesting, 'Why don't we take some of Nan's cakes for your dad?'

'A slice of apple pie might help,' Nan added.

'Do you think the chocolate fudge cake would be too messy to carry?' Harry asked jokingly.

They all laughed about it and then Joe finally announced, 'D'ya know what? I think 'e could be persuaded!'

'Can Joe come again tomorrow, please, please?' Harry begged, with Joe looking on hopefully.

'Of course you can. It's been a pleasure having you,' Bob replied, 'but I'll have to speak to your father about it.' The two boys cheered and then raced upstairs to Harry's bedroom to play computer games. When it was time for Bob to drive Joe home, both boys looked disappointed.

Joe was eventually driven off in Bob's car, accompanied by Harry, with a pile of foil parcels on his lap. When they returned about an hour later, Harry gave Nan a big hug. 'Thanks Nan,' he said. 'We've had a great time. It's so good to have a friend like

Joe.'

Nan thought it was a good sign when Bob referred to Joe's father as *Michael* instead of *Mr Robinson*. Harry was pleased that Joe could come again for tea and Nan was equally pleased to hear how much Michael appreciated her home baking. More importantly, Michael had agreed that he needed to accept their offers of help, for Joe's sake, if nothing else. Bob had persuaded him to see a doctor as soon as an appointment could be arranged and had promised to take him there himself.

Harry had plenty to tell his parents that night when they phoned and again they noticed the elation in his voice. He told them that Bob had called Joe *a truly amazing boy* and that Nan liked him too. Alice was delighted that her son had so much enthusiasm for this new friendship.

Nan was reluctant to tell her that Joe was by no means the perfect friend. She knew it was an unlikely friendship between two seemingly different boys. One boy was starved of friendship and the other was starved in the literal sense. The lure of her cakes was undoubtedly a factor in the beginning but their friendship was based on much more than that. They were kindred spirits drawn together by a common bond, a similar feeling of being neglected and abandoned by their parents. Whereas Joe reacted by craving attention, Harry reacted by becoming more withdrawn. As their friendship grew deeper over time, both boys were able to help each other to some extent. Joe showed Harry how to deal with bullying and helped bring him out of his shell. Harry acted as a moderating influence on Joe; while bringing Joe into contact with Nan and Bob was to change his life completely.

Chapter 6

At registration next day Joe was marked absent for the third day in a row. Joe didn't arrive till nearly half way through the first lesson which was French. The teacher was Mrs Phillips, a young and extremely attractive French lady with dark brown, shoulder length hair and beautiful, dark chocolate eyes. She was slim and petite with curves in all the right places. Like many French women she was elegantly dressed and wore high heels, nail polish and immaculate make-up. Although she was married to an Englishman, she still spoke English with a typically French accent that was both charming and sexy.

As usual Joe burst into the room in dramatic fashion. His face lit up and he did a double take when he saw the teacher. His mouth formed the letter 'o' and his face took on the stunned look of someone completely smitten. He carried on acting out his part, fluttering his eyelashes at her and saying in a heavy French accent,

''Allo 'Allo!'

Mrs Phillips may have been blessed with

good looks and a good figure but not a good sense of humour. She had no idea why the other pupils were laughing. She looked at him angrily and demanded to know his name and why he was so late.

Answering again in a heavy French accent he said, 'Listen carefully; I will say this only once. I 'ave been to the docteurs. I 'ave 'ad to sort out un petit problem….a man's problem.'

Mrs Phillips looked totally surprised and flustered, thinking Joe was about to divulge too much personal information. She had misinterpreted his words in exactly the way he intended. Waving him aside, she briskly told him to take a seat. Joe winked as he sat next to Harry on the front row. Harry found out later that Joe had in fact been to the doctors to make an appointment for his father, before Michael had the chance to change his mind.

The lesson resumed but Mrs Phillips made sure she kept a close eye on Joe, giving him the excuse to nudge Harry and whisper, 'She can't take her eyes off me!' Later in the lesson, when he had finished some written work, he looked back at her admiringly and asked, 'Miss, 'as anyone

ever told ya that ya 'ave beautiful eyes?'
She chose to ignore the question, which
was a mistake as he came back a few
minutes later with another one. 'Miss, are
they false?' The question earned Joe a kick
in the back of his chair from Poppy, who,
like the teacher, thought he was referring to
implants.

Mrs Phillips looked completely
flummoxed and could only stutter, 'I...I
beg your pardon. What did you say?'

''Ave ya got false... false.... eyelashes,
Miss?' Joe eventually elaborated, but the
smile which played around his mouth
suggested he was fully aware of the
ambiguity he had created.

She visibly breathed a sigh of relief but
Joe had one more question for her. 'Miss,
are ya married?'

She pointed to the ring on her left hand
and said, 'Of course I am.' Her face froze
in an icy scowl and she tried again to
ignore him. She was the only person in the
room who didn't find it funny, not even
when Joe declared that he was gutted.

By this time a clear pattern was
emerging which was repeated in all Joe's
lessons. He loved to take centre stage,

hogging the limelight with one comic performance after another. He played the class fool to perfection, disguising his true intelligence behind a mask of daft innocence. He took great pleasure in winding up teachers and shocking them with his outrageous, but funny comments. Whenever lessons became a battle of wits, Joe's sharp mind and quick wit meant that he was always more likely to win. Teachers were often at a loss how to handle him and he seemed to revel in their discomfiture. It was noticeable that he seemed to reserve his worst behaviour for female teachers. His mother's rejection of him had left him bitter towards women and until he met Nan, he had never had a good female role model.

However, even with female teachers, he never disrupted the whole lesson. Once he had made his mark, he tended to settle down and complete his work quickly. He was bright enough to know that the other pupils would soon turn against him if he denied them the chance of a good education. If anything the lessons were too easy for him and he resorted to entertaining the class to relieve his boredom.

He made up funny nicknames for all the

teachers, including the headmaster, and some had more than one nickname. Mr Atkinson was named *Batman* or *The Special One*, while Mr McMullen was known as *Big Mac* and Mrs Phillips was *Madame Petit Filous*. The nickname he chose for Miss O'Neil, *Frosty Knickers*, was uncannily similar to her staff nickname of *The Ice Queen*.

In a history lesson with Mr Pearson, Joe suddenly called out to him, 'Mr Pearson, ya remind me of someone I know. In fact you're the spittin' image of 'im.'

'Oh really? And who is that Joe?'

'Me grandad.'

Mr Pearson's face fell. 'Thanks very much! That's not very complimentary. I didn't think I was old enough to be a grandad!'

'Sorry sir.... but ya do look like 'im...except 'is bald patch doesn't shine like yours. D'ya put anythin' on it to get a shine like that?'

'No Joe, it shines more when people like you annoy me. Now get on with your work!' Joe often called him *grandad* and pretended that it had accidentally slipped out. Mr Pearson would have been even more annoyed if he had known that *grandad* had become his new nickname.

After only a couple of days, all of the dinner ladies, the clerical staff and every teacher in the school knew Joe's name. Even those who didn't teach him had certainly heard about him. Teachers often stopped Mr Pearson in the staff room or the corridor with complaints about Joe Robinson. The cookery teacher, Mrs Cartwright, told him that Joe had brought a tub of cream cheese and chives to make a cheesecake and suspected that it had been stolen in haste from a shop. One of the clerical staff also mentioned that some biscuits had disappeared from a tin in the office at about the same time that Joe was waiting there to have his report card checked.

There were times when Mr Pearson found it hard not to laugh at Joe Robinson, with his daring sense of fun and his cheeky charm. He had been on the receiving end of Joe's funny comments and had seen for himself the hilarious effect of his play-acting.

One morning he was about to mark Joe absent on the register when the door was noisily flung open and Joe hopped into the room on one leg, his body supported on crutches. Everyone looked surprised and Poppy asked with concern, 'Oh dear! What have you done to yourself Joe?'

'It's me ankle. I think I've broken it.'

Mr Pearson rushed from his desk and pulled out Joe's chair for him. 'Let me get you a chair.'

'Don't worry sir. I can get around great on these crutches. I'll show ya what I mean.' Using his crutches like ski- poles, Joe took huge strides back across the classroom towards the door.

Sensing an accident was about to happen, Mr Pearson advised, 'Joe, I don't think you should be doing that!'

But instead of resting his ankle, Joe wanted to show off some more of his tricks.

'Watch this!' Placing his hands on the arm rests, he hoisted himself off the ground and let his legs swing back and forth like a pendulum.

Mr Pearson warned him, 'Joe, stop that! You might fall and make your ankle worse.'

'No, it's fine, sir. I can even manage on just one crutch.' He laid one crutch on the desk and demonstrated how quickly he could hop on one leg across the room using the other crutch.

Then suddenly, to the amusement of everyone, Joe tucked the crutch under his arm and walked back normally to his seat. Even Mr Pearson saw the funny side and struggled to stop himself smiling.

'Joe Robinson,' he said sternly, 'you are unbelievable sometimes! Where did you get those crutches?'

'I found um in the boys' toilets propped up against a sink.'

'Didn't you think that someone might need them?'

'I just thought if they needed um they wouldn't have left um there.'

'A likely story! And anyway you shouldn't have lied to me about your ankle. You've only just come off report. Do you want another week of teachers' comments for every lesson?'

'Not really, sir.'

'Well, I suggest you take these crutches to the office now so that they can be reunited with their rightful owner. And make sure there's no more larking about!'

As 7S pupils left the room chattering and

giggling about Joe's antics, Mr Pearson had to admit that he had never met anyone like Joe before. He had developed a bit of a soft spot for him ever since he had questioned Joe in private about the reasons for his lateness. After explaining briefly in his usual chirpy way, Joe informed him that his dad was now getting treatment and soon wouldn't need his help. Joe had spoken coldly about his mother. She had left the day before his ninth birthday and since then birthdays always brought back painful memories. He had never spent any more birthdays with his brothers and sisters and had learned to make up his own fun without them. Joe had blanked out every memory of his mother, but the one thing that stayed in his mind was his mother saying that she had never enjoyed school.

Mr Pearson wondered what kind of mother would discourage their child in this way. But Joe didn't waste time feeling sorry for himself. With a huge grin he informed Mr Pearson, 'That's why I always make sure I enjoy meself at school!'

Chapter 7

Two inter-school football matches and three days of constant rain had left parts of the sports fields a quagmire of churned up mud. Mr McMullen decided these were perfect conditions to send 7S and 7T boys on a cross-country run. It would certainly test their stamina and fitness and, as he put it, *sort out the boys from the girls*.

This time Joe had avoided drawing attention to himself. He was wearing Harry's cast off trainers and PE kit and had arrived on time. Mr McMullen explained the route that involved three circuits of the fields surrounding the school, but before the boys set off he delivered a stern warning. 'In case any of you get any ideas, just remember lads, I know every trick in the book. So don't try any short cuts or think you can hide in the bushes and sit out one of the circuits. I'll be watching you all like a hawk, and some more than others!'

He had looked directly at Joe while he said this and Joe grinned back at him and shrugged his shoulders as if to say, *what are you looking at me for?*

The boys started off in a bunch but the narrow paths around the fields soon stretched the boys into a long line. It didn't take long for Harry and Joe to lag behind. Neither boy enjoyed running or any other sports activity and their lack of fitness began to show. To get their breath back they had to alternate running with walking and the spells of walking were gradually getting longer. They didn't have to worry about losing the route when the others disappeared out of sight; all they had to do was follow the trail of muddy footprints.

As they approached the end of the first circuit, Mr McMullen was waiting to urge them on. 'Come on you pair of big girls' blouses! Get a move on! I might have known you would be last, Joe Robinson!' He hurled similar abuse at them when they came around again after the second circuit. 'Get a move on you two! The others went past here ten minutes ago. My grandmother can run faster than you!'

Not long afterwards Harry noticed that Joe had slowed down and appeared to be hobbling. 'Are you all right Joe?'

'D'ya mean apart from bein' knackered?' Joe smiled ruefully. 'Actually

I do 'ave a problem. It's these feet of mine; they're a bit sore. They're just not used to runnin' in thick mud.'

'It might be the trainers rubbing your feet. You said they were tight when you put them on and you might have blisters.'

Joe tried to put on a brave face, despite the fact that each step was becoming agonisingly painful. Finally, he could bear it no longer and stopped to take off his trainers.

'Joe, what are you doing? You can't run in your socks!'

'Well, it's either that or me bare feet. I think ya were right. I must 'ave blisters and the trainers are pressin' on um.'

'Ok, but let's just walk the rest of the way,' Harry suggested, feeling guilty that his old trainers had caused the problem.

Joe knew instinctively what Harry was thinking and said cheerfully, 'Don't worry 'Arry. It's not your fault. I'll be all right on this soft mud. It's not like I'm runnin' on 'ard gravel.'

The two boys carried on walking and for once they were glad to see the figure of Mr McMullen waiting for them, as it meant their ordeal was nearly over. The last section the boys had to negotiate was at the bottom corner of the school fields. It was the junction of two paths and rainwater running down the slope from both directions accumulated there, making the area permanently boggy. A heavy plank of wood had been laid across the muddy pools to make it passable.

Mr McMullen started coming down the slope towards them, his voice already hoarse with shouting. 'Come on you lazy layabouts! I thought you'd got lost. The others are already having their showers.' Harry cautiously walked the plank and was told to hurry up and get back to school.

When it was Joe's turn, Mr McMullen's voice roared, 'Joe Robinson! What are you playing at, prancing about in your socks? You're not in a play centre now, you silly boy! No wonder you are so far behind. Get a move on across the plank!' With Mr McMullen watching from the other side, Joe should have guessed that the inevitable would happen. Whether it was the mud on Joe's socks or the mud on the plank caused by the extra traffic, or a combination of both, whatever the reason, Joe struggled to stay upright on the plank. He skidded on wet mud, his arms flailing frantically as he tried to regain his balance. His trainers flew out of his hand and landed in deep mud; two seconds later Joe slipped, overbalanced and fell face down beside them.

Mr McMullen's laughter was short lived when he realised his tracksuit bottoms had been splattered with large lumps of mud. He shouted at Joe again, 'You idiot! Look what you've done! Get out of that mud now! Who do you think you are? *Peppa Pig?*'

Joe had difficulty getting up and dragging himself out of the mud. By the time he retrieved his trainers he looked as if he had taken a mud bath. Mr McMullen scowled at him and continued to harangue him all the way back to the Sports Centre.

'Use the back entrance!' he ordered. 'I don't want you trailing mud through the front.'

The other boys had showered and changed and Harry was drying himself when Joe limped wearily into the boys' changing rooms, followed closely by the teacher. The sight of Joe caked in mud from head to toe was enough to halt all conversations. No one dared to laugh openly as Mr McMullen's face was livid.

'Get those filthy clothes off and then wait there, Robinson!' he barked, pointing to the entrance to the showers. The moment he disappeared out of the door the other boys' pent-up laughter burst out. Joe knew he looked a sorry sight but he was remarkably relaxed as he pulled off the muddy clothing clinging to his body. Harry obligingly scooped up the clothes and stuffed them into a plastic bag while Joe began singing, 'Mud, mud, glorious mud. There's nothin' quite like it for coolin' the blood....'

Mr McMullen must have heard him. He returned with a hosepipe in his hand and said, 'Here's something that will cool your blood. You need a lot more than a shower to get that mud off you.'

After adjusting the temperature controls, he pushed Joe into position and turned on first the cold shower and then the hosepipe. Joe was almost knocked over by the force of the water as Mr McMullen hosed off the mud from his body. When he was satisfied that he had taught Joe a lesson, he turned off the shower and stopped the hose. Joe was shivering uncontrollably and Harry had got a towel ready for him, but Mr McMullen wasn't finished with him yet.

'Where do you think you are going? You're not leaving the showers in this state, all messed up with your mud! You can hose down the walls and floor of the shower and after that you can mop the floor where you've left muddy footmarks.'

Mr McMullen stood with his arms folded, smugly watching while Joe hosed off the splashes of mud from the walls of the shower. He had nearly finished hosing the floor when the hose suddenly stopped.

'Hurry up and get it finished!' Mr McMullen shouted impatiently.

'I can't, sir. I'm pressin' the trigger but there's no water comin' out. I think the 'ose is blocked. There must be a kink in it.'

'Can't you do anything right? Let me look at it,' Mr McMullen muttered as he moved towards Joe.

What followed was the performance of Joe's life, one that would stay forever in the memory of those who saw it. Joe waved the hose as if trying to unblock a kink and, as Mr McMullen advanced, he pressed the trigger to maximum and the hose suddenly sprang into life. He gave a perfect imitation of someone frantically trying to regain control of the hose and in the process directing the full force of the water jet at Mr McMullen's head, or more precisely the top of his head. The blast of water was so strong that his toupee flew off his head and was swept along the floor of the shower looking like a drowned rat trying to escape down a drain.

All this happened in a matter of seconds and was accompanied by uproarious laughter. Joe quickly redirected the hose across the floor of the shower, at the same time crying out, 'I can't stop it! 'Ow do I stop it?'

With his bald crown exposed, Mr McMullen looked shocked and humiliated. He picked up his sodden hairpiece and marched out without saying another word. Joe stopped the hose and Harry threw a towel over him. The boys couldn't stop talking and laughing about it. Harry felt sorry for Mr McMullen, especially when Joe joked, 'I should've sprayed 'im with green paint and we could've called 'im *Shrek.*'

The bell for break had gone long ago and so the boys dismissed themselves. As they passed the male staff shower room the unmistakeable sound of the hairdryer led to another burst of muffled laughter.

Chapter 8

One teacher who never complained about Joe was Roddy Johnson. He got on well with Joe and had become a favourite with every class he taught. He was just as popular with the boys as he was with the girls. Like Joe, he was a born entertainer with a great sense of humour who could match Joe's quick repartee and good-natured banter. He recognised Joe's talent for acting and comedy and saw that he could hold the class in the palm of his hand. He realized that Joe was an intelligent, articulate boy, once you peeled back the layers of cheekiness and outspokenness that were his outward persona.

Roddy handled Joe by working with his comic genius and not against it. His methods may have been unorthodox but they worked. When Joe called Roddy, 'Miss,' accidentally on purpose, he reacted by putting on a girlie act. Fluttering his eyelashes and brushing back his long hair, Roddy replied in a woman's voice, 'Yes, my darling.' The class had laughed at Joe but they laughed even more as Roddy upstaged him.

Despite his inexperience, Roddy was able to bring out the best in Joe, especially in drama lessons where he excelled. When Roddy asked Joe and Harry to join the Drama and Dance Club, Joe in his usual impish way asked, 'What do I get for comin'?'

Roddy pretended to cuff him across the head and put on the funny voice of a very posh, outraged, elderly lady, 'You cheeky young whippersnapper! I don't know what's become of young people today!'

Roddy hoped the club would give pupils of different ages the chance to enjoy drama and dance together. Joe, Harry, Poppy and Rachel liked drama so much that they didn't need any persuading to take part in extra sessions. Lunchtimes were spent in merry mayhem with so much laughter, shouting and noisy collaboration that teachers nearby must have wondered if a riot had broken out. Every corner of the drama room was used by pupils practising their sketches in small groups or in pairs like Joe and Harry. Poppy and Rachel joined them for one of their sketches but they were mainly drawn to the street dance routines that were the ideal outlet for their tomboy energy. The Drama and Dance Club had become so popular that there wasn't enough floor space for all of the different groups to practise at the same time. When the street dancers had finished, it was their turn to watch as a group of eight girls practised a ballet routine that they had learned years ago in ballet classes. Their graceful dancing to the gentle music of *Swan Lake* couldn't have been a greater contrast to the heavy, thumping beat of the street dancers.

'I'm surprised that you and Rachel haven't joined that group,' Joe whispered to Poppy, whose face still glowed from her previous exertions.

She knew that he was teasing her and replied by elbowing him in the ribs and muttering, 'As if!'

'They look like they could do with another two dainty fairies,' Joe persisted. 'That fat one over there looks more like a plum puddin' than a *Sugar Plum Fairy!*'

'Stop laughing at them Joe!' Poppy said, trying not to smile. 'Anyway they're not fairies, they're swans and I'd like to see you do better!'

At that moment the fat dancer wailed, 'Sir, can you tell them lot to stop laughing at us! They wouldn't like us laughing at them!'

Joe had to bite his lip to stop himself from replying, 'Oh yes we would!'

Roddy gave him a disapproving look and warned, 'Stop it Joe, or you'll be out of that door!'

'Sorry sir, I was just thinkin' of an idea for a funny routine.'

'As it happens, I'm very pleased with what I've seen so far. I asked for as much variety as possible in dance styles and these girls have bravely provided that.'

The fat girl seemed very pleased with herself and gazed at Roddy with renewed adoration as he continued. 'Now that I have everyone's attention, I want to tell you all about an extra incentive to shine. Later in the term the school will be staging *An Evening of Music and Entertainment* for parents and children. The music department will of course provide the musical items, but the drama department, with the help of the Drama and Dance Club, will provide all the light entertainment.' Some of the pupils let out a cheer at this point and looked at each other with excited faces. Before they could ask any questions, Roddy went on to explain, 'We will be selling tickets to see the show, so the acts will have to be good. I can only choose the best acts, the ones that showcase your talents and work well on the stage. I can't have performers whose voices don't carry or who suffer from nerves and stage fright. The sooner you get used to performing on the big stage the better. We can't use the hall at lunchtime so it means extra rehearsals and auditions after school. Are you all prepared to do that?'

Most of the pupils either nodded or said, 'Yes', but some didn't seem so keen. Roddy knew that asking pupils to stay behind after school was a very different proposition from attending at lunchtime and he hoped to weed out some of the weaker, less committed performers.

Harry was one of those who seemed uncertain and Joe quickly noticed that something was troubling him. 'What's the matter 'Arry me old mate?'

'I'm thinking of dropping out of the Drama and Dance Club. I know I'm not a natural performer like you Joe and I think maybe drama isn't for me. The thought of performing on stage in front of a paying audience frightens the pants off me.'

'I'm sure ya would be all right,' Joe quickly replied, 'as long as ya don't poop yourself as well!'

Poppy pulled a face and said, 'Urgh! You are disgusting Joe Robinson!'

'Trust him to think of that!' Rachel exclaimed.

'Seriously mate ya can't drop out now. We're a double act, you and me. I couldn't do our sketches without ya as me straight man and I wouldn't want anyone else!' Then turning to Poppy and Rachel he said, ''E's great, isn't he? Tell 'im you two!'

'Honestly Harry, you're really good. You definitely shouldn't drop out,' Poppy confirmed.

'She's right,' Rachel agreed. 'You're not half as quiet and shy as you used to be and neither am I. I'm sure it's drama that's helped bring us out so it would be a shame to let Mr Johnson down now.'

'And me too!' Joe interrupted.

'You were never quiet and shy Joe Robinson!' declared Poppy, deliberately misinterpreting his words.

'Hey, Missie!' Joe said indignantly.

'You're not allowed to use *my* tactics on *me*!' They all laughed at this and then Joe turned to Harry and put an arm around his shoulder. 'Listen 'Arry, we're not lettin' ya drop out of the club. It 'ud be like breakin' up our little gang. The four of us get on so well together; it wouldn't be the same without ya, mate. We all 'ave to stick together, don't we?'

Touched by his friends' response, Harry smiled at last. 'No pressure on me then! Ok. Ok. I've got the message. Looks like I'll have to carry on, but I don't suppose Mr Johnson will pick our acts anyway.'

Harry was wrong; a few weeks later Roddy told them that three of their sketches had been chosen for the School Show. The two boys were in high spirits as they made their way to Harry's house that afternoon. They were still singing 'We're the ginger nutters, the ginger, ginger nutters, dada da da dada da da,' as they rushed through the front door and the hall, eager to tell their news. The singing stopped and the bubble of excitement burst abruptly when they found Martin and Alice sitting at the kitchen table with Nan and Bob having a cup of tea and some cakes.

Harry felt uncomfortable, as he had been dreading, and avoiding, this moment for months. His parents had never seen him in such a giddy mood before and he was afraid that they wouldn't approve of Joe. Like an anxious parent taking a naughty child to their first family party, he prayed that Joe would be on his best behaviour. 'Mum and Dad! I wasn't expecting you two at home today!' he managed to say.

To his relief his parents were all smiles and welcoming. 'We thought we would surprise you. So this must be Joe. We've heard such a lot about you,' Martin said.

'Oh dear! Not all bad I 'ope,' Joe answered, perfectly relaxed and not at all in awe of Harry's parents.

'We're very pleased to meet you at last. I know you come here often but we always seem to miss you,' Alice said, briefly glancing at Harry whose face began to redden. 'Nan tells me you've become one of her chief cake testers, so why don't you come and join us and try some of these chocolate brownies.'

The two boys quickly devoured the brownies and Joe delivered his verdict. 'Delicious! I think they're definitely up to standard. I bet ya miss Nan's cakes when you're in London!'

Martin and Alice laughed at this and Martin said, 'We definitely do!'

'Ya haven't told ya mum and dad ya news yet,' Joe prompted Harry.

'Oh yes, I nearly forgot. Three of our comedy sketches have been chosen for the School Show; one of them is with Poppy and Rachel, and Mr Johnson said that one of our sketches will *bring the house down*, whatever that means.

'It means it's very good, so well done you two. Your mum and I will definitely want tickets for the show, so when is it again?'

'12th November.'

'Right. I'll make a note of it in my diary,' Martin said, reaching for his i-Pad. 'Are you going to tell us about the sketches?'

'It might be better if they were a surprise. It won't be so funny if we've already described them,' Harry replied.

'Do you think your dad would like to come to the show?' Nan asked Joe.

'I'm sure he'd like to but I don't know whether he'd be able to manage it. He does seem to be gettin' better though, since he started takin' those tablets.'

'How about us coming along and bringing him?' Bob suggested.

Joe smiled back at them warmly, knowing that it would be the perfect solution. 'That would be great! I'd love 'im to see the show.'

'Well, it would be a shame if he missed it. I'll speak to him about it tonight.' He and Michael had become friends over the last few months and he always stayed to talk for a while when he brought Joe home and after the doctor's appointments. He was a good listener, as he had plenty of practice listening to Nan.

Martin and Alice met Joe several more times before the School Show and saw for themselves the close relationship between the two boys. Like Nan and Bob, they became very fond of Joe and appreciated how much happier their son had become. They also met Poppy and Rachel on a couple of occasions and were pleased that Harry had made such delightful friends. The girls were just as impressed with Staythorpe House as Joe had been.

'Wow, wow and double wow!' Poppy

declared when she saw the snooker room, her eyes darting around the room in astonishment.

Joe knew that Harry felt embarrassed and he quickly cut her short. 'Stop wowing, Poppy; ya sound like a dog barkin'! Let's get on with the game!'

Later there were further 'wows' from Poppy when she saw the selection of cakes Nan had made. 'Those cakes look wicked! I wish my Nan could make cakes like these.'

'They're the best cakes I've ever tasted,' Rachel drooled. 'I can see why Joe comes here so often!'

'Well I only eat 'em to keep Nan 'appy!' Joe said with a wink and received a playful tap on the shoulder for his cheek.

When the children ran upstairs to play the whole house seemed to echo with their voices, music and laughter. 'It's lovely to hear children enjoying themselves like that,' Nan remarked to Alice and Martin as they helped clear away after dinner.

'It's what a house like this was intended for,' Alice replied, 'but we're a bit concerned that it's a lot of extra work for you.'

'Especially when these children scoff so

many of your cakes!' Martin added.

'Oh, I don't mind. Bob's always here after school to help me and anyway you know how I love the baking sessions.'

'Harry does seem a different person since he's made these new friends,' Alice said. 'I never thought a quiet and reserved boy like Harry would ever have the confidence to appear on stage.'

'I think it's mainly Joe who's brought him out of his shell. He's such a livewire, but his sense of humour takes a bit of getting used to!' Martin admitted with a smile.

'I'm really looking forward to the School Show,' Alice said, 'but I just hope Harry's nerves don't get the better of him.'

Chapter 9

On the day of the School Show, Harry's anxiety had grown so much that he almost wished his parents weren't coming after all. Joe, on the other hand, was buzzing with excitement and couldn't wait to perform. With Poppy and Rachel's help, Joe managed to restore Harry's confidence by running through their sketches for the final time. Harry began to relax after this and they were all able to joke about putting on make-up for the show.

In the meantime Nan and Bob had a similar task of calming Michael's last minute nerves when they arrived to take him to the show. Michael had made a real effort, putting on his best clothes and Nan complimented him on his appearance. 'You scrub up well, Michael,' she said encouragingly.

'Thanks. Do you know this is the first time I've been out of the house in the evening since Mary left and that's nearly three years ago? I definitely wouldn't have gone out on my own.'

'Don't worry about it. You'll be fine,'

Bob reassured him.

When they arrived at the school they saw Martin and Alice waiting in the foyer. They were introduced to Michael and chatted amiably until it was time for the show to begin. After several items by the school choir, soloists, the school orchestra and solo instrumentalists, the audience was ready to appreciate the lighter entertainment provided by the drama students.

The first sketch was set in a café, represented by a few round tables and chairs and a large sign at the side of the stage displaying the name *Happy Café* and underneath *3 course meal and drinks for £10* written in large lettering. Joe appeared as a waiter with a grubby tea towel slung over his shoulder. He seemed to be full of cold and sneezed, coughed and wiped his nose on the tea towel as he straightened the chairs and prepared the tables. He picked up items of cutlery and breathed on them before polishing them with the tea towel. He then wiped some glasses in the same way and had started wiping another table when Harry arrived with his wife (Rachel) and his horrible, loud mouthed daughter

(Poppy).

Poppy looked around the café with a disgruntled expression and said rather loudly, 'It's a dump!'

Joe approached them with a big, false smile and said in a posh voice, 'Good evening sir, madam and ...*little madam*. Welcome to the Happy Café.'

'It doesn't look so happy to me!' Poppy said scornfully. Joe responded by clenching his fist at her and pulling a face when her parents weren't looking.

'Did you leave your car in our car park sir?'

'Yes I did,' Harry replied.

'Good. It's just as well you did as there are wheel clampers on the street outside waiting to pounce. Now if you would like to come this way, your table is ready.' He led them to a table and when they were seated he handed them menus.

As they studied the menus Poppy complained again, 'I still think it's a dump!'

'Well at least it's cheap and anyway this menu looks very impressive,' Harry replied.

Joe arrived at their table with a pad and

pencil and another big, false smile. 'Are you ready to order madam?'

'Yes I think I'll have prawn cocktail for starters and roast beef for my main course,' Rachel said.

'We've no prawns or beef left but you can have the cocktail without the prawns.'

'But that would be just lettuce and some sauce,' Poppy groaned.

'I'll have melon and chicken instead,' Rachel replied.

'No melon and the chicken's just run out,' Joe said with a shrug of his shoulders.

'That's what we should be doing!' Poppy said, rolling her eyes

'So what *do* you have for a starter today?'

'We have homemade soup.'

'What kind of homemade soup?'

''Ang on a mo, I'll just go and check the packet,' Joe replied in his usual accent.

'How can it be homemade if it's from a packet?' Poppy protested.

Joe returned and resuming his posh voice announced, 'It's pea soup,'

'Urgh! That sounds ominous in a place like this!' Poppy told her parents. This brought another scowl and a clenched fist from Joe.

'What do you have for the main course?' Harry asked.

'Well, let me see. No lamb, no pork and the fish is definitely off.'

'I can smell it from here,' Poppy said.

'We have a juicy sirloin steak,' Joe continued. Harry's face brightened before Joe added, 'but that will be an extra £20.' Harry shook his head. 'So that leaves us with our very special Hunters' Meat Pie.'

'Well it looks like it's three soups and three pies. Can you tell me what drinks are included in your menu offer?' Harry asked.

'You can have a full jug of water, but if you want something stronger, we have an excellent house wine.'

'That sounds good.'

'That will be an extra £20.'

'So the *drinks included* means water?'

'Yeh! What d'ya expect for £10?' Joe replied, his voice changing again.

'What a rip off!' Poppy said. 'I told you this place was a dump!'

'We'll just have water in that case,' Harry said resignedly.

Joe brought them a jug of water and three bowls of soup and Poppy immediately pointed to something moving in her soup. 'What's that in my soup?' she cried in horror.

'Don't worry. I'll get it out for you.' Joe took the soup to one side and fished something out. After wiping his fingers on the tea towel, he presented the soup back to Poppy and said, 'It was nearly dead anyway.'

'I'm not eating that when your filthy fingers have been in it! I don't know where they've been!' Poppy said, folding her arms across her chest.

'They're not filthy! I washed 'em this mornin',' Joe replied, his accent slipping again.

Harry and Rachel took one spoonful of their soup and immediately put down their spoons. 'That was disgusting. It tasted like dishwater,' Harry said.

'I wouldn't put anything past him, but when did you ever taste dishwater, dear?' Rachel asked.

Joe took away their bowls and when he brought the pies they prodded and picked over their food again with obvious dislike.

'This pie is just potato, onion and gravy. Have you found any meat yet?'

'No.'

'Neither have I.'

When Joe approached, Harry complained, 'There's no meat at all in any of these pies.'

'Really? You have been unlucky, but that's why we call it Hunters' Pie. Sometimes the hunters come back empty handed.'

'You might as well take away these plates. I think we've all had enough.'

'I've definitely had enough of this place!' Poppy snapped.

'Would you like to see the dessert menu, sir?' Joe asked politely while clearing the plates.

'Well, if it's like the rest of the menu, you might as well just tell us what we *can* have,' Harry replied with obvious annoyance.

Joe studied his pad and after crossing off several items, he announced, 'It looks like it will have to be meringue nest.'

'I don't know why he bothered bringing us menus!' Poppy said in exasperation. 'I can see why there aren't any other customers here.'

Joe brought them a dry meringue nest on

a plate and nothing else. When they tried to break it up by stabbing it with a spoon, the plates rattled and lumps of meringue flew onto the table and the floor. They had to resort to picking up the meringue nests with their fingers and after a couple of mouthfuls, Poppy shouted to Joe, 'I can't eat this without cream. It's making my mouth too dry!'

'Just a minute,' he replied and came back with a tall can of cream. He squirted a tiny amount on Poppy's meringue and she immediately moaned, 'Is that all we're getting? I can hardly see that!' To make her point, she bent over to examine it closely. Joe chose that moment to squirt extra cream and most of it ended up on Poppy's face.

'Oops!' Joe said laughingly. 'Is that enough cream for you now?'

As Poppy spluttered and wiped off the cream, Harry got up from the table. 'This is outrageous! Come on, we're leaving and don't expect us to pay anything for this.'

Joe quickly got out a phone from his pocket and made a call. 'Hi Mike, it's me. There's another car in the car park that needs clampin'. Can you do it now please?'

'You can't do that. That's illegal. I've been a customer here.'

'But not a paying customer and you're definitely not a happy customer. The notice in the car park clearly states that it is for the use of *happy customers.*'

'I thought it meant customers of the Happy Café.'

Joe shrugged his shoulders and said, 'It'll cost ya £170 to have the clamp removed, only after yuv paid ya bill of course, so altogether that comes to £200 ya owe me.'

'£200! I don't believe it. This is daylight robbery!'

Joe shrugged his shoulders again and said, 'I've not included tips in that, but to show ya there's no 'ard feelin's, I'll give ya a free ticket for our prize draw.'

'What's the prize?' Harry asked as he reluctantly got out his wallet.

'A free meal with drinks for four at the Happy Café.'

The sketch ended with Joe making another phone call and Harry and his family leaving the café.

The audience had chuckled throughout the performance and when the curtain closed they showed their appreciation with generous applause. The four friends smiled happily as they took their bow, pleased that their sketch had been such a success.

After the interval, the audience enjoyed a lively street dance routine by a large group of boys and girls, including Poppy and Rachel and further comedy sketches. In one of them Joe and Harry played newsreaders whose faulty autocue meant that they kept reading the wrong lines with comical effect.

The final act of the show began with the orchestra playing Tchaikovsky's well known music from *Swan Lake*. It heralded the arrival on stage of a line of four girls wearing long white tutus, white tights and ballet shoes. Their arms were crossed over at the front and their hands joined as they performed a specially adapted version of the *Dance of the Cygnets*. The girls danced superbly considering the difficulty of the dance and the fat girl at one end of the line surprised everyone with the lightness of her feet. They moved across the stage from side to side, each time varying their steps and head movement and yet still keeping in perfect unison.

When they crossed the stage for the third time, the eyes of the audience were drawn to a fifth dancer who had tagged on to the line. He had ginger hair and thick glasses and was dressed in a long white tutu like the girls, but instead of ballet shoes and tights he was wearing trainers and red football socks pulled over his knees. The sight of Joe clumsily trying to copy the steps of the others, while being yanked across the stage by the fat girl, brought a huge reaction from the audience. The wolf whistles and cheers increased when they reached the other side of the stage and another ginger haired dancer, similarly dressed, joined the other end of the line. Within seconds they had created chaos, completely messing up the synchronization and turning the dainty *Dance of the Cygnets* into the *Dance of the Drunken Swans*. The audience loved it, especially when a change of direction and a sudden jerk from the fat girl sent Joe sprawling across the floor. As Roddy had predicted, the act *brought the house down* and earned the loudest applause of the night.

It was a fitting finale and Martin and Alice, Nan and Bob, and Michael all enjoyed it as much as the rest of the audience and were very impressed with both boys' performances. Martin and Alice were amazed at the transformation of their previously shy and withdrawn child and knew that they had Joe to thank for this.

At the end of the show, the headmaster was waiting in the foyer to receive the congratulations of the parents as they left. He was dressed to impress in his gown and came over to Martin and Alice as they waited for Harry. It was only after talking to Martin Cowper- Smyth that he made the connection between the M.P. and Harry Smyth. He had no idea until that night that Harry was in the same form as Joe Robinson, or worse still, had become his best friend. Mr Atkinson disliked Joe and had never forgiven him for undermining his authority in the smoking incident. He considered Joe an undesirable influence on the son of such a prominent member of the community and he made up his mind then and there to separate the two boys and break up their friendship as soon as he could.

If he had known what Mr Atkinson was plotting, Joe wouldn't have been in such a good mood after the show.

'You did really well Joe. I didn't realise you were such a comedian,' Michael remarked as they drove home in Bob's car. 'Mr Johnson told me after the show that you might become the next Peter Kay.'

'Well, if I do end up like Peter Kay I'll take ya all for tea at the Ritz and we'll have some proper cakes!' Joe said with a smile.

Nan pretended to cuff him across the head. 'Right, that's the last cakes I'll make for you, my lad!'

Joe laughed, 'Sorry, ya know I'm only jokin'. I'll tell ya what, if I do any concerts, I'll reserve front row seats for ya.'

'No thanks,' Nan answered quickly and then explained, 'not the way Peter Kay takes the mickey out of his Nan!'

Chapter 10

The following week Joe inadvertently played into Mr Atkinson's hands by getting involved in a fight with two other boys. It happened in the playground when the two boys from 7T started making fun of Harry and Joe for wearing make-up and tutus for the School Show. Harry and Joe ignored their taunts but the boys seemed determined to pick a fight and targeted Joe in particular.

One of them pushed Joe and sneered, 'So you think you're the next big comedian eh? Well I think you're nothing but a great big fairy, prancing about the stage with the girls.' He followed this by punching Joe in the stomach and saying, 'I bet he squeals like a girl as well.' The other boy pushed and punched Joe in the back so that he ended up sandwiched between them.

'Leave him alone!' Harry shouted, trying to pull one of the boys off Joe. But Joe was more than capable of defending himself. He swung his elbow at the boy behind him and at the same time lashed out with his fist at the boy in front of him. Unfortunately, his fist caught the boy's nose which started to bleed heavily, and the splashes of blood on his white shirt made the injury look much worse than it was.

The teacher on playground duty rushed to the scene, alerted by the gathering of spectators and the cries of *Fight! Fight*! He quickly pulled them apart and soon all three boys were hauled before the Head of Year. The other boys blamed Joe for starting the fight and the injury seemed to back their claim that Joe was the aggressor. Miss O'Neil brushed aside Joe's version of events and warned all of them that there was never any excuse for fighting in school. She informed them that she would have to consult Mr Atkinson about the matter, but it was highly likely that they would be suspended. She finished by asking them to report to the headmaster's office immediately after school.

Later that afternoon the three boys were led into the headmaster's office by Miss O'Neil and stood sheepishly in a row before the headmaster's desk. Miss O'Neil took a seat alongside Mr Atkinson who leaned back in his chair and looked disdainfully at each boy in turn. After lecturing them on the school's policy of zero tolerance of fighting, he solemnly told them, 'I have decided to suspend all three of you from school for three days. Don't think for a moment that a suspension is the same as a holiday. It is a very serious matter and will be on your school record. The school governors will have to be informed of it. Any further breaches of school discipline will lead to a longer suspension and eventually could lead to permanent exclusions. Do you know what that means?'

'Yes sir,' they chorused.

'In simple terms you could end up being removed from this school if you carry on like this. Over the next three days you need to think very carefully whether you want to stay here or not.'

He paused dramatically for a moment as if he wanted his words to sink in, and then he handed each boy a sealed envelope. 'I want you to take these letters home to your parents or guardian explaining the reason for your suspension and asking them to make an appointment to see me in school before you return.'

Joe opened his mouth to speak, 'Sir...'

But Mr Atkinson silenced him immediately. 'Don't you dare interrupt me! I've not finished with you yet!' With a jerk of his head he signalled to the other boys, 'You two can go now.' Glancing sideways, Joe saw them smirking at him as they left the room.

'Joe Robinson,' he began slowly and emphatically, 'I am absolutely sick and tired of you! You are being suspended today for fighting, but I can tell you now that I don't like your friendship with Harry Smyth. You are a bad influence on him and I can't afford to have you leading him astray. If he gets into trouble, his father will blame the school and the reputation of this school is very important to me.'

Joe detected more than a hint of satisfaction in the headmaster's voice as he came to his conclusion. 'For this reason, I have decided to move you to 7D when you return to school. If you continue to cause trouble there, I may have to move you again, but perhaps by then you will have been thrown out or you will have asked for a transfer to another school. Do I make myself clear?'

'Yes, sir.' Joe had listened in stunned

silence and for once he couldn't find a witty answer or pretend that he didn't care. He knew by the steely look on the headmaster's face that any protest would be futile. His mind was in such turmoil that he didn't explain that his father might have a problem making an appointment.

Harry had waited for Joe and was understandably shocked and upset when Joe told him the news. 'He can't do that! He can't split us up! From what you've said it sounds like he wants you out of the school, not just 7S,' Harry cried.

Joe tried to cheer Harry up as they walked back to Staythorpe House. 'I think 'e's 'ad it in for me ever since I told 'im I was doin' a poo…. instead of smokin', or it could have been the crutches or Shrek's toupee that 'e 'eard about.'

A smile hovered around Harry's mouth for a moment. 'I know what you're trying to do, but it won't work. I'm still gutted!'

'Listen 'Arry we can still be friends. We can see each other after school and at break and lunch time. I'll make sure I don't get in any more trouble…or at least don't get caught!'

Harry couldn't be consoled. Nan and

Bob had never seen him so miserable and even Joe found it hard to be cheerful. He didn't know how his father would manage an appointment with the headmaster and he was dreading giving him the letter. He knew he would be disappointed, especially after the euphoria of the School Show. Neither boy had much appetite for their tea and Bob wisely decided to take Joe home early so that he could face the music sooner rather than later.

When Harry's parents phoned that evening, Harry told them tearfully, 'It's not fair! Joe didn't even start the fight. The other two boys started punching Joe first and he was only defending himself. They believed the other boys when they blamed Joe because one of them had a nosebleed. No one asked me what happened, so I didn't get the chance to stick up for Joe. I don't see why Joe should be moved to 7D as an extra punishment. Mr Atkinson just wants to break up our friendship.'

Martin and Alice let Harry continue his angry tirade and when he had finished there was little they could say to make him feel any better.

Lessons seemed to drag the next day and

the whole class missed Joe's lively presence. Harry obviously missed Joe most of all. He was subdued and quiet and hardly spoke to anyone the whole day.

Late in the afternoon, Mr Atkinson received a surprise visit from Martin Cowper-Smyth. He greeted Martin warmly and the two men shook hands.

'Ah, Martin. Nice to see you again. What can I do for you?'

'I spoke to Joe Robinson's father earlier this afternoon and he agreed that I should speak to you on his behalf. You are probably not aware that Joe's father suffers from depression and has been virtually housebound for nearly three years. He has only recently started to receive treatment. Joe has had to cope with the aftermath of his mother leaving and taking all his brothers and sisters with her. Any other boy would have used that as an excuse to go off the rails, but instead he has taken on the sole responsibility of caring for his father as well as the shopping, cooking and washing. I'm not trying to paint Joe as a saint, we all know he's not that; but I hoped you might see him in a different light.'

'I admit I wasn't aware of all this.'

'I believe Joe has been suspended and moved to another form.'

'He has indeed,' Mr Atkinson affirmed. 'We have a very strict policy on fighting.'

'I can understand your decision to suspend Joe for fighting, although Harry is adamant that the other boys started the fight and Joe was just defending himself. I'm surprised that no witness statements were taken as there was no opportunity to verify Joe's version. You wouldn't want to be accused of victimisation, would you?'

Stung by the criticism and put on the defensive, Mr Atkinson looked for a scapegoat. 'Miss O'Neil dealt with the matter so I would have to speak to her about that.'

'Did Miss O'Neil take the decision to move Joe to another form?'

Mr Atkinson avoided giving a direct answer by saying, 'We've been concerned about Joe's undesirable influence on your son for some time and we thought the friendship should be discouraged. Joe is an attention seeker who often disrupts the class so I would have thought we were doing your son a favour by moving the boy.'

'Quite the opposite, Mr Atkinson. Harry is devastated. Joe is his first real friend and my wife and I are more than happy to encourage the friendship, not discourage it. We think that Joe Robinson is the best thing that's ever happened to our son. Harry has been a completely different person since he met Joe. He's become much happier, confident and outgoing and separating him from Joe would do more harm than good. I'm not trying to tell you how to run your school. I wouldn't presume to do that. But I would like you to reconsider your decision to move Joe from 7S.'

'I can see why you went into politics, Martin. You can be very persuasive. I never imagined you would react like this.'

'I've cancelled all my appointments and travelled from London this morning so I think that gives you an idea how strongly I feel about it.'

The headmaster shifted uncomfortably in his seat. He was reluctant to change his mind but he knew Martin had influential friends in the Education Authority and he didn't want his reputation tarnished.

'I'll have to speak to Miss O'Neil about this, as I was acting on her recommendation,' he lied. 'But in view of what you have told me I suppose we could let Joe stay in 7S.'

'Thank you very much. Harry will be delighted.'

Chapter 11

'Thanks dad! Thanks, thanks, thanks! I can't believe you did that for me. You're the best dad in the world!' Harry's words echoed in Martin's mind for a long time afterwards, pricking at his conscience. He knew that he hadn't been *the best dad in the world*, far from it. Harry had jumped up and down with joy when he had heard that his father had persuaded Mr Atkinson to change his mind. He especially appreciated the fact that his father had missed work and travelled from London to achieve this. It was a turning point in their relationship because it was the first time Martin had put his family before his work; and he felt good about it afterwards.

As he travelled back to London on the train he regretted spending so little time with Harry and knew that there were not many years of his son's childhood left. He began to wonder whether he should step down from his parliamentary committees so that he could devote more time to his family. It was highly likely that his party would lose the next General Election so realistically his parliamentary career was doomed anyway. The idea was tossed around his head as relentlessly as the rhythm of the train; and the nearer he got to London the stronger his feeling that this was the right thing to do. When he discussed it with Alice, she was in complete agreement.

A few weeks later Martin had another opportunity to get closer to his son. Harry had mentioned that it was Joe's birthday on 3rd December and that he had never enjoyed a birthday since his mother left on the eve of his ninth birthday.

'Did you say that Joe supported Liverpool rather than Manchester United?' Martin tried to sound casual, but he still managed to arouse Harry's curiosity.

'Yes he does, but why are you asking?'

'I've been offered the use of an executive box at Anfield on 3rd December and I wondered whether Joe might enjoy that as a birthday treat.'

'He's never been to a football match before so I'm sure he would love it. But what do you mean by an *executive box*?'

'It's a private room with a balcony overlooking the pitch and waitresses serve a 4 course lunch with drinks before the match and drinks at half time. The executive box we've been offered has been rented for the season by Read's Haulage and the owner of the firm, Alan Read, owes me a few favours.'

'Why isn't he using it himself on 3rd December?'

'Before the fixture list was published, his daughter chose that day to get married, and he could hardly tell her that he was off to Anfield instead.'

'Some might!' Alice joked. 'But isn't it a bit cold to get married at that time of year?'

'Not in Barbados though!' Martin laughed.

'And would you be able to come too, dad?' Harry asked hopefully. He still wasn't used to his father's changed priorities.

'Of course I will. I wouldn't miss it for the world. It'll be the first football match we've watched together too. We can have up to 10 people so we'll have to think about whom to invite.'

'I think Joe would want to ask his father, his grandad and Bob, but the pupils we're friendly with are all Manchester United supporters so there's no one else. I can't wait to tell Joe. He will absolutely love it, especially the food and drink part!'

'If you like you could just tell him that we've got tickets for the match and the executive box could be a surprise,' Martin suggested.

'We would have to promise him a pie and chips or something before the match to stop him having lunch beforehand,' Harry added in a conspiratorial tone. He smiled happily at his father as they enjoyed plotting the surprise together. 'Dad,' Harry began tentatively, 'there is one last thing. Joe told me that he had never had a birthday cake in his life. Is there any chance that we could smuggle one into the executive box and have it as a surprise after the match?'

'I'm sure that could be arranged. I know someone who makes exceedingly good cakes!' Martin replied jokingly.

Nan said that she would be delighted to make Joe's birthday cake and agreed to make one in the shape of a football pitch.

'Why don't you and mum come along too?' Harry asked, with a hint of pleading in his eyes. It would be nice if we were all together so you could sing *Happy Birthday* as well. Have you seen the sample menu dad downloaded from the Liverpool website?' Like his father, Harry could be very persuasive when he wanted something. Nan and Alice decided that, even if they didn't enjoy the football, they would certainly appreciate the food and drink, and they agreed to come along.

'We would still have two places left so I was thinking that we could ask Uncle Gareth and Noah. We haven't seen them for ages and I'm sure they would enjoy the outing,' Martin suggested.

'That sounds great, dad. I'm really looking forward to it!'

Uncle Gareth was Martin's brother and he and his wife, Joan, lived with their two children, Noah and Isabel on their farm in North Wales. Noah was 7 years old or *nearly eight,* as he liked to tell everyone and got on well with Harry when they came to visit in the summer holidays. He was always very protective of his 4-year-old sister and knew that she was disappointed that she couldn't come to Liverpool.

'Sorry Isabel, it's for boys only, but I'll bring you back a present to make up for it,'

Noah consoled her. 'Anyway we need you to make a birthday card for Harry's friend Joe.'

Isabel's face brightened; she liked nothing better than an excuse to get out scissors, card, glue and glitter and she wanted to start immediately.

Uncle Gareth's work on the farm kept him busy throughout the year and he rarely had a day off work. After checking that his wife could manage without him, he was delighted to accept Martin's invitation.

'What's that noise in the background?' Martin asked in the middle of their telephone conversation.

'Oh, don't worry about that. It's only Noah jumping up and down on the wooden floor. He's so excited!'

Saturday 3rd December was a bitterly cold day, with a forecast of snow later that night. Joe, Michael and Joe's grandad were all dressed in six layers of clothing to keep out the winter chill. Harry smiled to himself when Joe sat down beside him in the back of Martin's car, but he didn't want to spoil the surprise by telling him that he wouldn't need to wrap up so much. They travelled in convoy, with the others following in Bob's car. Martin thoughtfully switched off the heater as Joe unzipped his coat, revealing another jacket underneath.

'I've got another four layers under this coat and jacket,' Joe informed them. 'Three jumpers and a red T-shirt to bring them luck. I've even managed to put on two pairs of trousers and two pairs of socks.'

'Did you remember your red underpants to bring them luck?' Harry giggled.

'I wasn't goin' to mention that 'Arry, 'cos you told me to be on me best behaviour.'

'I didn't say that!' Harry laughed again. The friendly banter between the two boys continued for most of the journey.

Harry gave Joe his birthday card and told him they were going to the Liverpool Superstore at Anfield first to buy his present. He leaned towards Joe and told him confidentially, 'You can choose anything you like. Dad told me he doesn't mind paying, whatever the cost. He just wants you to have your best birthday ever.' Even through Joe's thick glasses, Harry could see his eyes misting over.

'It's already that!' Joe mumbled, turning

his head away to hide his tears.

When they arrived at Anfield and parked the cars, Joe was too busy talking excitedly to Harry to notice Bob carrying a large canvas laundry bag. It had been chosen to transport Joe's cake as it needed to be kept both flat and hidden. Nan had even draped a couple of scarves over the see-through cake container to keep it from view.

At the Liverpool Superstore, where they had arranged to meet, they quickly spotted Noah and Uncle Gareth. Noah raced towards Harry and greeted him like a long lost brother.

'You've grown such a lot since I last saw you!' Harry exclaimed. 'You're nearly catching me up! It must be all the milk you drink on the farm. Your hair's grown a lot too! I think we need the sheep shears on this mop of yours!' Harry tousled Noah's blond hair affectionately and Noah smiled. He liked Harry and wished he lived nearer so he could see him more often.

Joe and his family were quickly introduced to Uncle Gareth and Noah who wished Joe a *Happy Birthday*.

'Isabel's made a birthday card for Joe, even though she doesn't know him,' Noah informed them. He produced a large pink envelope from a carrier bag and presented it to Joe. Joe smiled and Noah warned him, 'You'll have to be careful with it because I think she went a bit mad with the glitter!'

As Joe cautiously opened the card, a sprinkle of glitter, sequins and silver stars fell to the floor. 'Tell Isabel it's the best birthday card I've ever seen,' Joe said, admiring her sparkling creation before putting it back in the envelope.

'She wanted to come,' Noah confided, hopping from one foot to the other, 'but I told her she was too young and it was a boys' only outing.' Alice and Nan exchanged glances and smiled.

Uncle Gareth shook his head and said, 'He's been bouncing around like this since I told him!'

Noah was a delightful, happy-go-lucky boy, full of boyish exuberance. Like his father, he rarely strayed far from the farm and the trip to Liverpool was a real treat for him. The prospect of seeing his first game of football with his cousin had raised his happiness levels to overflowing. 'We've brought you some freshly laid eggs from the farm. We know how much you like them,' Noah enthused, looking at Harry who was glad that he didn't add *with your soldiers*. 'And there's some butter and cheese and some of our organic vegetables as well,' Noah continued, pointing to a cardboard box which his father had rested on the floor, between his legs. Tal-y-Cafn Farm Deliveries was printed on a large label on the outside and poking its head out of one corner was the top of a large stalk, covered in sprouts.

'Dad didn't realise we would be parked so far away, otherwise we could have popped the box in the boot of Uncle Martin's car,' Noah explained.

Martin and Alice thanked Gareth for the farm produce and then it was time for Joe to choose his present. The three boys eagerly set off on the first of several circuits of all the merchandise. Joe eventually chose a Liverpool mug. Harry frowned and shook his head. 'Oh no you don't! You've got to have more than that. I know you really wanted a Liverpool shirt.'

'Let Nan and I buy the mug,' Bob stepped in. 'We wanted to get Joe a present.'

'And we'll get the shirt,' Martin decided.

'Come on Joe, I know you are a fan of Steven Gerrard so you can have his name and number on the back.'

As well as the shirt, Martin bought the three boys Liverpool scarves and a teddy for Isabel. Harry, Joe and Noah emerged from the shop with huge grins on their faces.

'Are you all ready for something to eat now?' Martin asked.

'I'm always ready!' Joe cheerfully admitted.

Martin led the others through the main entrance and into the plush surroundings of the foyer where there were a few raised eyebrows and bemused expressions among the men in suits and the well-dressed ladies. Read's Haulage had never entertained such an odd assortment of guests. There were two roly-poly Michelin men, one of them wearing a flat cap, a Michelin boy, a man carrying a large red-checked laundry bag and another man carrying a farm delivery box which obviously included sprouts!

Martin's rag-tag party followed him across the foyer and down the thickly carpeted corridor, leaving a diminishing trail of red glitter all the way to the executive box. Michael and Joe's grandad had already guessed, but Joe had no idea of the surprise until he stepped into the room and let out a huge 'Wow!' His eyes surveyed the red-carpeted room with its long dining table impressively laid for ten people, the red, high gloss kitchen and small bar area at one end and the balcony at the far end with an uninterrupted view of the pitch. Pictures of Liverpool legends hung on the walls alongside one of the Read's Haulage logo.

Everyone laughed, as Joe in his inimitable way asked, 'So is this where we 'ave our pie and chips?'

Joe's father and grandad began taking off their extra layers of clothing and his grandad explained that he had insisted on all the layers after suffering from frostbite during the war.

But Joe couldn't miss a comic opportunity. He took his clothing off in full striptease fashion, swaying his hips suggestively and waving each layer of clothing above his head, accompanied by the famous chorus of *dada…da…da, dada…da…da* After taking off his extra pair of socks, Joe's finale was to move the zip of his trousers up and down a few times before eventually revealing the other pair underneath.

Martin laughed along with the rest at Joe's performance and said, 'There's never a dull moment with this lad around!' Even the waitresses smiled as they took orders for drinks and starters. There were several choices for each course with wine for the adults and soft drinks for the boys. They all enjoyed their meal and every time Harry looked at Joe, he seemed to be bursting with happiness.

'You haven't even seen the match yet. They're playing Chelsea so it should be a close game. Would it spoil things if Chelsea won?' Harry asked.

Joe gave the perfect reply. 'Even if they lost 0-6, it'ud still be me best ever birthday!' He then turned to Martin and said, 'Thank ya so much for all of this.'

The boys were presented with match programmes after the meal and they went out onto the balcony to read them and watch the stands slowly filling up. Joe proudly put on his football top over his remaining jumper and they joined in some of the singing holding their scarves above their heads.

The adults relaxed in their comfy chairs, talking and enjoying the hospitality of the executive box. Joe's grandad enjoyed telling war stories and Michael seemed completely at ease. They didn't join the boys on the balcony until the match was about to begin.

It was an exciting game with Liverpool coming back from a goal down to win 2-1. Harry, Joe and Noah jumped up and down with delight when Liverpool equalised and hugged each other when Steven Gerrard scored the winner.

After the match, the waitresses served more hot drinks. The three boys sipped their hot chocolate on the balcony, savouring the atmosphere, their voices hoarse with singing *You'll Never Walk Alone*.

'I don't want this birthday to ever end,' Joe told Harry.

'But we've not finished with the surprises yet. Turn around and look!'

Joe saw Bob advancing towards him carrying the football pitch birthday cake lit with flickering candles. Everyone sang *Happy Birthday* while Joe admired the cake and then he was urged to blow out the candles and make a wish. Martin took photos to record the occasion and Joe asked him to take one of the cake before it was cut. He couldn't believe that Nan had made it.

'You've really surpassed yourself with this one, Nan!' Alice declared as everyone enjoyed a piece of cake. Nan smiled contentedly and was about to say something when there was a knock at the door and to everyone's amazement Steven Gerrard walked into the room.

He smiled shyly and in his familiar Scouse accent asked, 'So whose birthday is it here?'

'It's Joe's,' Harry said, pointing to his friend who was so star struck he was left speechless and could only smile bashfully at his hero. Harry nudged him to let him know he wasn't dreaming.

It seemed to do the trick for Joe suddenly said, 'Great goal, Stevie!'

Steven didn't seem to mind the familiarity; he just smiled and said, 'Thanks.'

Steven's appearance was almost surreal. He stayed for only a few minutes, but long enough to sign the match programmes and Joe's shirt, as well as posing for photos with the three boys.

Later that evening, before he went to bed, Harry asked his father, 'Did you have anything to do with Steven Gerrard's visit?'

'I made a request through a friend of a director but he couldn't give any guarantees, as Gerrard's normally quite reserved.'

'Thanks dad. Joe's face was a picture, wasn't it?'

'So was yours!' Martin joked. Harry and his father had never felt closer.

'I'm so glad you like Joe,' Harry said. 'Having a best friend is the best thing in the world.'